RAIN AFTER THE FIRE

Lorenz Qatava

ISBN: 979-8-5731141-9-4

DEDICATION

This book is dedicated to those whose lives were suddenly unsettled by the Almeda fire on September 8, 2020, and especially to the families of four individuals who lost their lives, including Donald Schmidt and Violet Lobdel. It also pays tribute to the brave firefighters and first responders who risked their lives to protect and serve others. #SouthernOregonStrong

CONTENTS

ACKNOWLEDGMENTS

The author thanks Liz Silver, Karim Premji, and Mark Kelly for their encouragement and support in the writing of this book. He thanks Tim Learmont and Peter Kupfer for invaluable editorial support. He also is deeply appreciative to William Lawson and the students of the creative writing program of the Osher Lifelong Learning Institute (OLLI) at Southern Oregon University.

CHAPTER 1

ASHES FROM ASHES

Evan and Sheila blankly stared out over the ashes of the home that they had made together over the past six years.

All that remained was a sea of bone-white ashes, ghostly planks of jagged charred wood, the dust-covered form of a brick chimney, skeletal metal remains of appliances, pieces of the white picket fence, and two cracking red ceramic tree pots that once framed the entrance. Somewhere out there in this massive ash heap were the myriad fragments of their lives – wedding photos, a family bible, holiday ornaments, a charm bracelet, first date concert ticket stubs, a scale model of the Taj Mahal and everything, big or small, that they ever owned.

Just forty-eight hours ago Sheila stormed out of the house that once stood there, her cheeks stained with tears, reeling from the wretched, disgusting betrayal that she had just heard confessed from Evan's lips. As she drove away from that house on that cloudless morning, she could hear fire engines in the distance, but nothing seemed out of the ordinary as she drove down North Main Street. "Where's the fire," she thought and, how could it be worse than the one happening in her life right now?

Her mind was racing to figure out her next step. She had heard of women who had tolerated such a betrayal, but her Lutheran upbringing made it hard for her to reconcile this with the vows that she had exchanged at the altar with Evan six years ago. "Damn him," she thought.

Soon she was on the freeway, heading north, but not sure where she was going. She just needed to be anywhere away from the college sweetheart, who was now a monster that she didn't recognize. The buzz of helicopters overhead drifted into her conscious mind and distracted her momentarily from the rage she was feeling. She pulled off at the Biddle Road freeway exit and drove to her friend Karen's house. Karen was a middle-aged divorcee and would know just what to say and could tell her what she needed to do next. At least she could have a good solid, gut-wrenching cry with Karen.

There was no answer at Karen's door. She texted her and waited, but got no reply. She could feel the heaviness of her body as she slumped down on Karen's stoop. "Breathe" she reminded herself. In her mind, life with Evan was over, and she needed to formulate a plan to move forward without him in her life. She heard more helicopters and sensed the faint smell of smoke in the air.

"One of those forest wildfires must be pretty close," she thought. Her cell phone buzzed, and she thought it was Karen, finally calling her back. Instead, the screen read, "Mandatory emergency evacuation alert for Talent Oregon. All residents must evacuate the area immediately."

A few hours later, she found herself in a serpentine line at the Jackson County Expo Center emergency shelter. A silver-haired woman took her name and gave her forms to fill out. "Oh yes, Mrs. Vickerson," she said, "I checked in your husband, and he is waiting for you in Section C, with your cat. Such a lovely gentleman."

Sheila was physically and emotionally exhausted and didn't have the energy to explain her situation to this kind, but beleaguered Red Cross volunteer. What would she say, "that faithless fool is <u>not</u> the man that I married."? Instead, she just silently took the blanket, pillows, and clamshell filled with fast food and proceeded to the assigned area. Evan sat on a small cot next to hers.

"Honey, I'm so glad that you're OK. I am so sorry." Sheila cut him off with a look and a wave of the hand and turned her back to him as she sat on her cot, just four feet away. She didn't want to hear any of it. No more sorries, no more lies.

She moved to a nearby table to eat in silence and show her contempt, distracting herself by focusing her attention on her neighbors, who stumbled around like zombies, waiting for any news about what had happened to their own homes and when they could go back. Sharing stories about where they were that morning when the fire started.

She recognized the librarian whom she saw every Saturday at the Scrabble group and the waiter at the pizza place where they went on Fridays. But their faces were not the faces she had seen at the library or the pizza parlor. They were faces lined with worry and fear, of dread for the consequences of a day from hell when they fled their homes with little more than the clothes on their backs, not knowing if they would ever return to the ordinary lives that they knew when dawn rose on that fateful Tuesday morning.

Throughout that night and the next, she had tearful talks with neighbors, Evan's parents, trauma counselors, legal advisors… all of them offering whatever support she needed to get "back to normal." She did not tell anyone about the firestorm that had incinerated her relationship with Evan.

Evan was her college sweetheart, the man she sat up late nights quizzing for the bar exam. The man for whom she prepared and hosted dinners and parties for his clients and work associates. He was the man for whom she gave up her dream of a tech career so that they could settle in this peaceful southern Oregon hamlet. The man she made vows to, cared for, depended on, and loved.

Sitting on the cot, she remembered that morning when she started screaming hysterically as Evan tried to explain that he was in love with an actor he met on a camping trip. For almost a year, he had deceived her. He said that he didn't want to hurt her, but that this "passion" rendered him helpless to escape his true self. Did it have to be the morning of the same day when hell briefly escaped the netherworld to consume her house, her garden, and the entire town? She couldn't stop her mind from trying to calculate when it all went so terribly wrong. When did he stop loving her, and how did she miss something so obvious as a sexual attraction to someone of the same gender. How does that even work? Did her inability to bring a child to term somehow make her less of a woman, and was that why he would reject the female form? She had so many questions.

Two anxiety-ridden days passed until they could return to see what was left of their home. She left the emergency shelter after one night and stayed with her friend Karen until the insurance agent called and set up a time that they could be escorted past the roadblocks to the street where they once lived.

The putrid stench of toxin-filled smoke still lingered in the air as Evan and Sheila stood side by side, but far apart, on the sidewalk in front of 315 Strawberry Lane. They were drowning in their individual grief as they looked upon the graveyard that was once their happy home at the end of this cul-de-sac.

The chatty Mutual Life agent was busily producing form after form on his clipboard and asking a barrage of questions about their worldly possessions. Where was their bank account or safe deposit box? How old was their car, their refrigerator, what models?

Evan stopped an answer mid-sentence when his cell phone rang. He quickly moved away from Sheila, but she could clearly overhear him consoling the man who had been responsible for ending their marriage and who had caused such sudden and irreparable pain. What she overheard from the conversation was that he was in the hospital and that his family wanted privacy. "Serves him right," she thought.

The insurance agent completed his inquiries with Sheila, gave her his business card, and drove away. Sheila looked over at her pathetic husband standing several feet down the sidewalk and knew that at this moment of intense shared grief, it was the other…" lover" that he was comforting.

Standing there in the donated and ill-fitting green dress that had belonged to some stranger, she wondered if she could steal that woman's life as well, instead of the tragedy she was living at this very moment. She paused at the surprisingly intact picket fence that she had painted gloss white, took a deep breath, and removed the wedding band from her ring finger. With all the strength she could muster, she tossed the band as far as she could into the smoldering heap.

Evan pocketed the cell phone and turned his attention back to Sheila. She had barely spoken ten words to him, civil or uncivil, over the past two days. Their eyes met momentarily, and they could see tears streaming down each other's cheeks. Then they both turned their gaze back to the ash heap before them. *Evan and Sheila blankly stared out over the ashes of the home that they had made together over the past six years.*

Slowly at first, then more rapidly, raindrops began to fall.

CHAPTER 2

WANDERING, WONDERING

In April of 2019, Evan and Sheila took a trip to India with the hope of re-energizing their fragile marriage. Neither of them had ever traveled abroad and, in the aftermath of the stillborn death of their first child, Evan decided that this was something that would provide a welcome distraction and an opportunity to bond. They chose the Golden Triangle tour of northern India from a catalog for its combination of historical and exotic sites that could be seen over a short period of time. For three weeks, they boarded a series of buses, trains, and planes across northern India in a group of Americans led by a local tour guide. The ancient city of Khajuraho was the third of six stops on the itinerary.

As Evan entered the brightly-lit coffee shop inside their hotel in Khajuraho, he looked around for others in his Smartours group, someone else who may have also chosen to skip the optional trip to the tiger sanctuary. After a morning of climbing the ancient temples and deciphering the erotic karma sutra carvings, he needed some downtime and left his wife on her own to explore with the group.

He spotted one of the tour group members sitting alone at a corner table, just finishing her lunch. He had never said anything beyond a polite hello to her over the past ten days. Still, he was intrigued by this diminutive middle-aged, modestly-dressed woman traveling all alone on the Golden Triangle tour. She always sat on the front row of tour buses and never joined the group for drinks, dinners, or shopping.

After asking permission to join her table, he asked how the trip was going for her so far. She quietly responded, "Fine," then after a short pause added, "but all the smells, the crowds, and the clatter get to me sometimes. Seeing the hordes of begging children who gather every time we get off the bus just breaks my heart." Evan nodded in agreement.

"Have you traveled with Smartours before?" he asked.

"This is my third trip this year," she responded. It was only April. He soon learned that she had taken almost a dozen similar three-week excursions in the past year, always alone in a large group in some exotic locations in Asia, Africa or South America.

After telling the waiter that he just wanted coffee, he focused on this woman, a full foot shorter than him. She would have been invisible in most places, assumed to be a humble domestic worker, her unkempt greying hair and wrinkles indicating a hard and troublesome life. So different from the thirty other globe-trotting, middle-class tour participants.

Remembering his manners, he introduced himself, and she responded, "Yes, Mr. Evan, you are Sheila's husband, from Oregon, and you are a lawyer. You don't have any kids. She talks a lot, but you don't." He was impressed with her candor and astute observations and slightly embarrassed that he didn't recall her name, but couldn't figure out a polite way to ask now.

"Wow, we maxed out a couple of credit cards to be able to come to India for three weeks. How can you travel so much?" She paused, smiled, and said with conviction, "It's my inheritance." He wasn't sure if she meant that she had inherited money or if travel had a larger meaning for her. She proceeded to tell him one of the most remarkable stories he had ever heard.

I was born in Marseilles in the south of France to a drug-addicted mother who couldn't take care of me. When I was twelve years old I was taken from her and put in an orphanage. After three years of bouncing around foster homes, some bad, some not so bad, I was adopted by a couple who had two boys around my age. The father was a diplomat, and our family soon was moved to Rio de Janeiro for his work.

When I was almost seventeen, the oldest of my adopted brothers forced me to have sexual relations. He also blackmailed me to keep it secret. My mother took me to the doctor when I began to show the first signs of pregnancy.

When he learned I was pregnant, my very strict adopted father became very angry and wouldn't believe that his son was responsible. It was horrible and I ran away to fend for myself on the streets of Rio. While working as a waitress at a cafe, I met a lonely and naïve American frat boy, and we had an affair that lasted for about a week. After several weeks of love letters back and forth, I lied and told Howard that I was pregnant with his child and needed money. To my surprise and horror, he immediately flew to Rio, and we were married the next day. We returned to Miami together on New Year's Eve of 1989.

Howard's wealthy parents were skeptical that I was pregnant by their son, who reluctantly agreed to have the marriage annulled and then convinced me to have the baby boy adopted at birth before I could even hold him or see his face. As part of our agreement, they helped me get citizenship, supported me to get a nursing degree, and paid for a small apartment.

After I graduated, I found work as the office assistant to two gay doctors in an exclusive private practice in Miami Beach. The doctors were also lovers, who shared a beautiful mansion overlooking Biscayne Bay. Their personal life was only known to a small group of close friends. They insisted that I move from my tiny apartment into their casita guest house. I worked for them for nine years and eventually, I managed not only the medical practice, but the household accounts as well. I was like a member of the family.

In September of 2001, we traveled to New York City, where the doctors were to meet with their legal and financial advisors about combining their substantial assets to get married. I had never been to New York and was thrilled to tag along and play tourist. On the morning of their appointment, we took the subway downtown together, and I split off to take the Liberty Island ferry. As the ferry approached the enormous green statue, a woman next to me began screaming hysterically and pointed back at the Manhattan skyline. We all looked up as a jet airplane flew into the World Trade Center. The ferry passengers stood there frozen in horror as another plane struck the other tower, bursting in flames and smoke, and moments later, both towers came crumbling down.

The doctor/lovers arrived early for their 9:00 am appointment on the seventieth floor of Building Number 1. Several days later, I returned to Miami Beach, not knowing if they had survived. The Miami Herald laid on the doorstep of their mansion, with the headline "Miami Beach Doctors Among the 9/11 Jumpers." I was distraught at finally learning the fate of my good friends and patrons and went into a deep depression. As the weeks went by, I stayed in the main house waiting to hear from one of their families but knew that their families had rejected them because of their sexuality. There were no memorial services, no obituary, no gathering of friends. Their office sat vacant. It was as though their lives had disappeared into thin air.

For the past eighteen years, I have lived in their house, paying all the household bills out of their offshore accounts, keeping the outward appearance of normal occupancy, and traveling as often as possible. Each time I returned to the house on Flamingo Circle, I am afraid that the government or some relative would confiscate everything. But each time, the key works and the cavernous home is empty.

Evan was riveted and couldn't believe how matter-of-factly she recited this sad, tragic story, as though she had told it hundreds of times before to total strangers in group tours.

His coffee had turned cold and he could hear the group in the lobby returning from the tiger sanctuary. He signaled the waiter to bring the check. His legal mind went to all the ramifications and entanglements that her precarious situation could cause her, but he was on vacation from the office and let those thoughts float away.

"That's, uh, a pretty amazing story," he finally said, "What will you do if you return and the house has been claimed?"

She paused, looking down at her coffee cup, as though the answer were there, then looked up and said with a smile, "I guess I would just keep wandering."

CHAPTER 3

RIVER OF ASHES

Early the next morning, the road-weary group assembled at the Khajuraho airport to board a commercial airplane for Varanasi. Evan had shared the woman's incredible story with Sheila and another couple in the group over dinner. They stole furtive glances as she boarded the plane, as though she was a notorious celebrity, traveling undercover.

They arrived in the ethereal spiritual mecca of Varanasi in the afternoon, checked into the hotel, and gathered in the lobby with their guide, Krishna, a rotund middle-aged man with a thick beard and, inexplicably, traces of a New Jersey thicker accent. To get to the Ganges, they had to take a bus toward downtown, switch to horse-driven carriages, and then finally walk ten blocks through crowded streets to the embarcadero. At the dock, they rushed to get on the rickety chartered boat before sunset.

The boat sailed out to the middle of the Ganges, where they were surrounded by a hubbub of humanity, bombarding all the senses. Young boys splashed about in the filthy waters as fishing boats, canoes, and water taxis buzzed around them. The rhythm of drums and sitar music wafted through the air. Large bedsheets, hand washed in the river water, hung from clotheslines on wooden poles on the shore.

Krishna, seated comfortably in a lotus position in the center of the boat full of curious American tourists, explained the ancient mystical meaning of the Ganges River for devout Hindus, Muslims, Jains, who make lifetime pilgrimages to this sacred place refreshed with waters flowing from the peaks of the Himalayas. Krishna directed the group's attention to the vast farmland on the quiet west side of the river where the sun was just beginning to hover over the horizon, then back to the river's bustling east side where dozens of red clay ritual crematoriums dotted the hillside. As if on cue, men dressed in all white robes opened doors, stepped onto small balconies holding aloft large urns containing the just-cremated ashes of recently departed male relatives. They held each urn high above their heads, chanted a few phrases, and ceremonially tossed the ashes into the river.

Krishna gave a short lecture on karma and beliefs about reincarnation. Each passenger was given a small votive candle placed on a bed of lotus flowers and he invited them to gently place the lit candle on the surface of the water in memory of someone dear to them. When the mystery woman asked for a second candle, Evan overheard Krishna respond to her by name and he learned that her name was Wanda.

This ceremony on the river was a small quietening moment of calm amid the constant din, a refuge from the insistent commotion of Indian life. Evan put his arms around Sheila as she lit her candles and called out the names of her parents as she released the candle into the water. He looked over at Wanda, whose cheeks glistened with tears as her two lit candles floated silently away from the boat joining with the others.

As the boat sailed back to shore, he noticed young monks in saffron-colored robes marched in single formation up the hillside to their monastery for evening prayers. Krishna orchestrated a reverse operation back to the hotel by foot, carriage, and bus through Varanasi's hectic streets.

Once he got back to the hotel, Evan looked for Wanda, but she had been first to get off the bus and hurried off to her room. He left Sheila in the hotel restaurant just as soon as dinner was finished and went to the business center to do a Google search for '9/11 Jumpers.' He vaguely remembered it but soon learned details about an estimated 200 people had made the unthinkable choice to leap to certain death rather than die in the burning skyscrapers. He scoured the list of names, followed links to newspaper articles, but couldn't find any reference to two doctors from Miami Beach.

After another day in Varanasi, the group traveled on an uncomfortable noisy train that was first class by Indian standards to the city of Agra. After a short time to settle in, Krishna assembled them on the beautifully manicured lawn at the entrance to the Taj Mahal for a dramatic recounting of the history of India's best-known World Heritage Site. He left them to explore the grounds and mausoleum on their own.

Evan was mesmerized by the groups of women in colorful saris gliding gracefully in front of the gleaming white marble of the magnificent Taj. Sheila paged through the brochure, reading about the symmetry of the four minarets leaning slightly outwards from the central onion dome.

Wanda appeared out of nowhere and asked, "Mr. Evan, would you take a picture for us, please?" He took the compact digital camera from a twenty-something couple from Los Angeles who were using this tour as their honeymoon. He took several photographs of the trio with the young couple beaming, arms around each other on the "Princess Diana bench," and Wanda standing slightly apart. Behind them, the reflection of the setting sun provided a colorful illusion as it transformed the stark white marble into ever-changing shimmering pastels.

As he gave the camera back to Wanda, he gave her his business card and thanked her for sharing her story with him. He hoped that she would return the gesture and give him her full name or something that would provide more clues to her identity. But, she just thanked him, gave a sly smile and walked away.

Looking out from the Taj Mahal steps, Evan and Sheila shared a tender embrace as the moon began to rise and reflect on the tranquil waters of the Yamuna River.

"I love you, sweetheart," Sheila said.

"I love you to the moon and back," Evan replied, kissing her gently on her lips.

"This year has been so horrible with losing the baby," she paused as the sadness rose in her.

"The doctor said that we could try again, and wouldn't it be wonderful if we conceived him or her right here in India. I think we may have done it already." Evan's reply made her smile.

"We could name her Mumtaz after the Mughal princess entombed just beneath us." She turned and gazed out over the shimmering river reflecting the moonlight. "This has to be the most romantic spot on the planet. Would you spend the next twenty-seven years and your entire fortune building a monument to me?" But, as she spoke, Evan's eyes drifted elsewhere. Sheila turned and saw Wanda and the L.A. couple looking at a marble inscription a few feet away.

"Will you stop obsessing over that darn woman," Sheila implored, "If I had to worry about another woman, I would have hoped that she would be a lot younger and a lot prettier."

"I'm sorry, honey, there is just something about her story. I spoke with Krishna and he confirmed that she is indeed from Miami, and she was on his company's trip to Tanzania last month." At that moment, Krishna called out, "OK, everybody, time to go!"

That evening Evan came down to the ornate lobby of the Royal Pashima Hotel to board the bus for a theater performance with the group, a live play about Shah Jahan and Mumtaz, the beautiful bride for whom the Taj Mahal was built. Wanda sat at a small draped table with her back to him, talking to the bug-eyed Los Angeles couple. To settle this mystery once and for all, he needed to get the doctors' names or her ex-husband's family name, something he could use for an internet search. He paused, close enough to the trio to overhear Wanda telling the couple the exact same story he heard in Khajuraho. At that moment, Sheila tapped him on the shoulder, beckoning him to hurry to join the group for the play.

"Gnarly ma'am, that's so epic!" Evan overheard the young newlywed exclaim as he reluctantly was being pulled away by Sheila to join the group. "Can we buy you a burger, ma'am? I saw a McDonald's just a few blocks from here."

They arrived in Delhi for the final stop of the three-week journey across northern India. The group shared a lavish farewell dinner at a restaurant on the night before departure, following a full day of touring Old Delhi and New Delhi. It was sad to say goodbye to some of the new friends they had made and to reflect on the memories they had shared along the journey – the Khajuraho temples, the Ganges, the Taj. Wanda was mysteriously missing from this gathering, as was her contact information on the mimeographed roster that Krishna distributed.

The group members stepped off the bus at Indira Gandhi International Airport, said their goodbyes, and dispersed to their different airline counters, and then onward through security inspection to wait in lounges to board various planes for the long journeys to Dallas, Chicago, Atlanta, Los Angeles, or New York. Evan and Sheila showed their travel documents to clear security and collected their hand luggage.

Evan was browsing the liquor shelves at the duty-free shop to kill some time when he spotted Wanda at a distance, ticket in hand, about to board a flight. He ran towards her and called her name across the vast terminal, hoping to finally confront her about her story's veracity and solve the mystery once and for all. On hearing her name, she turned, gave him a half smile and a wave, opened her mouth to speak, but thought better of it. She turned away and disappeared onto the gangway. Disappointed and exasperated, he looked at the lighted information board above the gateway, wondering where she was going. The sign read, "American #105, Destination: Anywhere."

Sheila ran after Evan on the concourse of the Delhi Airport. He was still breathing heavily after running out of the duty-free shop chasing Wanda and holding an unpaid bottle of Chivas in his hand. When she caught up to him, she asked, "Honey, are you OK?"

"It's Wanda," he said, "she just boarded that flight with the destination of 'Anywhere.'" Sheila followed his outstretched hand to the sign.

"You mean that flight to Atlanta? I imagine that she transfers to Miami from there. Come on, you silly man, you'll get arrested and we will miss our flight over this obsession of yours."

Evan limply followed her towards the gate, and, for the first time in the past three weeks of eating all kinds of strange spices and foods, he felt physically sick. He dashed off to the nearest men's room, just in time.

CHAPTER 4

THE FAMILY THAT PRAYS TOGETHER

Evan's adopted younger brother Eddie met the couple in the international arrivals area of the Portland airport. Their parents, Barb and Jerry had been cat-sitting for them while they were in India, and they needed to collect Mr. Peeps before making the five-hour drive back to Talent. Eddie, dressed in baggy black combat fatigues, was monosyllabic during their drive to the ranch-style house in Tigard, a Portland suburb.

There was a fourteen-year gap between Evan and Eddie, who was adopted as a four-year-old, right after Evan left for Oregon State University. They had never formed a fraternal bond, and Eddie was often moody and distant. Evan worried about the emotional toll it was taking on his parents, who should have been enjoying their golden years.

"It's our favorite daughter-in-law and her husband. We missed you guys," Barb exclaimed standing in the doorway as she gave huge mama bear hugs to the bleary-eyed couple. Eddie marched defiantly around them, his face frozen in a scowl, and went straight to his room and closed the door.

"What's going on with him?" Evan asked, "Is he still messing around with those right-wing groups?" For the past six months, Eddie had been spending most of his time in his bedroom, connecting online with groups like Incel (involuntary celibates), the Oath Keepers, and other anti-government political groups. He had even gone to a Patriot Prayer rally in Portland but only stood on the sidelines.

"He says they're just patriots. I don't think they do any harm. Good for him!" Jerry said.

They put their bags away and freshened up and, after a little downtime, Sheila joined Barb in the kitchen to help prepare dinner. Evan joined his father in the den, where he was watching a Trail Blazers basketball game. He gave a small grunt when Evan entered the room, and there was silence until a commercial break.

"So how did those Indian people treat you, son?" Jerry asked. Evan told him about the palace in the middle of a lake that they had seen in Jaipur, the elephant ride, the colorful Holi celebration where everyone threw colorful dust on each other. Jerry "uh-hummed" occasionally, watching closely for the game to start up again. At the next commercial break, he turned to Evan and said, "You heard they upheld that liberal Supreme Court homo marriage decision? See what happened to this country when they put a commie Kenyan in the White House?" Evan knew better than to take the bait to get into a political discussion with his father. He was delighted to hear Barb call out, "Everybody at the dinner table… now!"

Jerry was a proud man who, with just a high school education, had worked his way into the middle class with his job as a technician at a plumbing company. He worked long hours and moonlighted as a handyman to give Barb the comfortable life that she desired. He was a quiet man and always dutifully agreed with Barb. The only time he even mildly disagreed was when she insisted on adopting a sickly Korean child when they were in their forties and Evan was finally off on his own, but Barb had prevailed. His tastes were simple and he was perfectly happy to have a few brews, watch sports, or lose a few bucks in an occasional poker night with his work buddies. Unfortunately, neither of his sons had much interest in sports or socket wrenches. Once they became adults, he only took a passing interest in their lives.

Barb and Sheila filled the dining table with overflowing platters of fried chicken, bowls of corn pudding, green bean casserole topped with almonds, and popover rolls as the men arrived and took their traditional seats. They held hands and Jerry blessed the food. Eddie started loading up his plate like a man who had not eaten in weeks. Barb shared the latest gossip about family members, and Jerry sprinkled the conversation with headlines he heard on Fox News.

When dinner was finished, Sheila excused herself and went to the guest room. She returned with gifts from their Golden Triangle tour, a colorful sari for Barb, an ornately-carved leather belt for Jerry, and a pair of traditional Rajasthani royal puppets for Eddie. Mr. Peeps hopped up onto Evan's lap as if to ask where his present was.

The couple settled in for a melatonin-induced night's sleep. At 3:00 am, Evan was wide awake and headed to the living room to not awaken Sheila. As he walked down the hallway, he could see that the door to his brother's dark bedroom was ajar and could just make out his silhouette typing in front of the light of a computer screen. He gently tapped on the door, entered the room, and sat on the bed. The Rajasthani puppets lay next to Eddie's keyboard.

"Kinda late to be up on the computer, kiddo. What's so important?" Evan asked.

"I'm talking to my friend Mochi in Korea," Eddie replied.

Eddie was a self-confessed virgin, who was more or less adrift and rudderless in life as he approached his twenties. As the only Asian student in his classes, he was constantly teased and bullied because he didn't fit the smart whiz kid stereotype, and he was too husky to engage in martial arts. After high school, he briefly had a job at Voodoo Donuts and shared an apartment in downtown Portland. Unfortunately, his roommate was heavily into drugs and he got Eddie into using opioids, which he became addicted to. It landed him in rehab and back in his parent's home. There, he played video games all day, read manga comic books, and went to recovery group meetings.

Eddie had been adopted as an infant from a South Korean orphan agency by parents who brought him and his twin sister back to Portland. The adoptions cost them over $30,000. The father lost his manufacturing job soon after they returned from Seoul and was unable to find work for over a year. In the meantime, Eddie had a series of childhood illnesses that required expensive medical care that put the family on the brink of bankruptcy, and the father was drinking heavily and threatening to kill the son. In desperation, the adoptive mother contacted her church friends Barb and Jerry and asked if they could take one of the children until they got back on their feet. A few weeks later the woman and her daughter left her abusive husband in the middle of the night. The father was arrested and the mother disappeared. The Vickersons formally adopted Eddie so that they could be legal guardians for his medical care, but the mother never returned.

"Can I ask you something?" Eddie said while idly playing with the puppets. "What does it feel like to be normal? You are so good at everything, with your perfect job and your perfect wife."

Evan took a deep breath. "My life isn't so perfect, Eddie. But what's important is what <u>you</u> want <u>your</u> life to be. Decide that and make it happen. Mom and dad won't be around forever. When I was in India, I learned a lot about karma. Do you know what that is?" Eddie shook his head. "It's a set of Hindu principles, and one of them is that of cause and effect, where intent and actions of an individual influence the future of that individual. Essentially, what we do in this life has consequences in the next life. You control your own destiny, Eddie. There is so much ahead for you."

"If you say so," Eddie lamely replied as he stood up, dropping the puppets on the floor, "I think I want to go to bed now."

CHAPTER 5

OLD PATTERNS RETURN

Early the next morning Evan and Sheila packed up the car and Mr. Peeps for the long road trip from Tigard back to the town of Talent. Talent is a small suburban community at the southern-most tip of Oregon, situated between the quaint liberal tourist town of Ashland and the larger conservative blue-collar city of Medford, where most of the county population reside and the location of the busy regional airport.

Sheila soon realized that very little of their Strawberry Lane home life had been changed by their journey and their lives quickly returned to a familiar pattern. Evan had only one day before returning to the law office and found a huge backload of work. Sheila spent a few days reliving her Indian adventures, sorting and scrapbooking her 700 pictures, and trying her hand at some recipes that she had learned during the day at the Delhi Cooking School. She nurtured, weeded, and revived the long-neglected plants in her garden and caught up with the reality shows that she followed.

Mostly, Sheila daydreamed about India and just wished she was somewhere else. Evan came home exhausted each evening, and even on the weekends, he seemed far away. Friday night was their "date night" when they would go to The Grotto pizza parlor, and she tried to keep things light, but he was usually distant and moody.

Sheila adored her in-laws. Her own parents had died a decade ago right after college graduation, her mother of breast cancer and her father of a massive stroke, almost exactly six months later. She was an only child to her parents, who had her late in life. They spoiled her with their attention and bought her anything she wanted. It was as though she was filling a void in their own relationship. They also instilled in her a strong Lutheran work ethic. She was good at math and science and graduated valedictorian of her class in St. Paul, Minnesota. She went on to study computer science at Oregon State University, which is where she met a shy law student named Evan. One of her sorority sisters needed another girl to go on a double date with her and a guy that she met at a mixer. Sheila was immediately smitten with Evan, who shared her passion for learning and hard work. They were married the following year in a traditional wedding at his family church in Tigard. Over the years, memories of her birth parents faded away, and Barb and Jerry became more like her parents than Evan's.

After six years of living in Talent, Karen was Sheila's only friend. Karen was almost forty and very pretty, though she had let herself get a bit thick around the waist. They met in a Weight

Watchers class. Sheila admired Karen for being a single mother, raising her lovely daughter alone after a bad marriage. Jennifer was living at home with her mom in Medford while pursuing a biology major at Southern Oregon University. She was the perfect daughter, very polite, popular, and smart.

She envied Karen for having a child on whom she could lavish her attention. She never wanted anything as much as she wanted to have a baby. She quit the tech job that she had worked so hard to get to reduce her stress level. She watched her ovulation cycles to find the best times to have sex. They met with a fertility specialist. Barb added the birth of a grandchild to the intentions of her prayer circle. After almost four years, the obstetrician finally gave them the news that Sheila desperately wanted to hear. She was carrying Evan's child. She knew that this seed would be the panacea that would forever bond them together. Evan was happy to give his parents a grandchild, but not sure he would be such a great dad.

Tragically, in the first trimester, something went terribly wrong, and she lost the baby, a girl that they named Amanda. Evan held and consoled Sheila night after night as she sobbed uncontrollably. She began withdrawing into despair, despite Evan's promise that they could try again when she was ready. After a year of counseling and therapy, she slowly began to function again and move through the motions of married life. That's when Evan suggested the international trip.

Once they were back home from abroad, Sheila continued to get weekly calls and emails from tech headhunters. Women with her skills as a software designer and systems engineer were in high demand. But she convinced herself that Evan needed her to support his career and that being a mother was her true calling in life. They bought the house with cash, money she inherited from an elderly aunt, so they got by very well on Evan's meager salary. A job for her would be an unnecessary distraction.

One Saturday per month Sheila and Karen volunteered at the animal shelter in the neighboring town of Phoenix. It was where Sheila had found and adopted Mr. Peeps. The place was always chaotic with the constant din of barking and meowing. They had to walk, bathe, and feed the animals. It seemed to benefit the volunteers as much as it did the homeless pets.

When Sheila arrived on that first Saturday morning in June, Karen and Jennifer were already in line waiting for their volunteer assignment for the day. The coordinator asked if they wanted to do dog washing or kennel cleaning. Karen quickly replied that they wanted dog washing.

"No, I want to do the kennel cleaning." Karen and Sheila looked at each other in surprise to hear that Jennifer wanted to do such an unpleasant chore, but agreed to let her to split off for the day. Once they separated they realized that what Jennifer was really interested was in the other volunteer doing kennel cleaning –

a fellow student named Jarrod, a "Ken doll" type who was a football player, a senior and in her chemistry class at SOU.

It took all the strength of both of them to control the frisky dogs as they lathered them up and rinsed them off one by one. The biggest challenge was trying to get a big towel and blow dryer near them before they could shake water all over the room. After a couple of hours, they were soaking wet and exhausted but laughing and joyful. They went to the break room for a cup of coffee, before finishing off the final half dozen dogs awaiting their spa experience. Sheila couldn't wait to share her big news with Karen.

"Remember what I told you that Evan said when we were on the steps of the Taj Mahal?" Sheila asked, "Well, I missed my period in May and took the test again this morning. He was right, we're pregnant!"

CHAPTER 6

INDEPENDENCE DAZE FIREWORKS

Independence Day was Sheila's absolute favorite holiday. She loved the festive parades, the traditional summer foods, and, most of all, the fireworks. There were many celebrations all over southern Oregon, but none better than the one in nearby Ashland. She was up early on the morning of July 4th, preparing the dish that she had seen in Family Circle Magazine, which she was taking to the McSmiths for their annual holiday celebration.

"It's a hot one out there, honey," Evan said as he returned from a five-mile morning run along Bear Creek Greenway. "Mmm. That smells good." Although it was a holiday, he still had a little bit of work to finish up before they headed over to the Ashland parade that started at ten. He showered, got dressed, and pulled some contracts from his briefcase to review. Sheila came into the den dressed head to toe in red, white, and blue, with a giant flag striped patriotic hat. "Oh, my goodness, aren't you the spirit of independence!" he said.

They arrived on Main Street just as the sidewalks were filling up, with family groups sitting in lawn chairs, toddlers upfront. There were flags everywhere, and people were standing shoulder to shoulder, with cameras, and cellphones in hand to capture that picture-perfect moment to post on Instagram. At the stroke of ten, military jets flew over, signaling the beginning of the parade. The Ashland High School marching band's trombones and tubas blared out Sousa tunes, uniforms crisp, batons twirling high. The parade went on for over an hour, with everything from a bicycle riding City Councilman to cowboys dancing in pink tutus to bagpipers and mariachis. It was an homage to everything that makes small-town America special. Sheila was more and more thrilled by each contingent as it went by, jumping up and down like a schoolgirl.

After the parade, they followed the crowd as they surged into Lithia Park for a civic program that included the traditional reading of the Declaration of Independence and patriotic tunes by a brass band in the city bandshell. They quickened their paces as they passed between rivaling pro-life and pro-choice protesters and stopped at the booths to support different community groups.

That afternoon, Sheila finished her covered dish to take over to the McSmiths for the holiday party. They arrived around 7:00 pm and had to park a couple of blocks away because there were so many cars for the party. There were already over two dozen smartly dressed couples packing the deck. The modern house was spectacular, something right out of Architecture Digest, set high on a hill up Mountain Avenue with a view of the Rogue Valley and Grizzly Peak.

Roger McSmith was the founder of the law firm where Evan worked, with many civic and political connections throughout the area. Sheila gave her platter to Roger's wife and complimented some new artwork in the living room as they walked together to the dining room. Evan looked around the room to see that most of his work colleagues and their wives were there, along with a smattering of politicians that he recognized and a few new faces that he did not. Sheila rejoined him outside on the deck, where Evan had gotten a beer for him and white wine for her.

"Oh, thank goodness there is someone our age here. Hello!" A loud, shrill voice came seemingly out of nowhere, "We were getting afraid that there just would be stuffy old lawyers. I'm Darlene, and this is my *husboy*, Gregory." Sheila was a bit taken aback by the loud-mouthed woman in a peasant dress with lavender-tinted hair and the man in a Hawaiian shirt with brightly colored tattoos on his arm.

"I'm Sheila, and this is my *husband*, Evan. Evan works at the McSmith and Paramus law firm, which is sponsoring this event. I suppose he isn't stuffy yet."

"Gregory is an actor at the Oregon Shakespeare Festival." Darlene couldn't resist joining in the one-upmanship. "He is currently performing the lead in Romeo and Juliet," she paused for effect, "...that would be <u>Romeo</u>. But, let's be real, this party sucks and the Fourth is a crock of hooey. I mean, really, we build billion-dollar jets while people live in tents on the street. We only came because the host, whoever he is, is a big OSF donor."

"Hmm, I don't think we have ever been to <u>that</u> theater," Sheila said dryly, "So nice to meet you. Enjoy the party." She took Evan's arm and led him away. Evan wished that they had chatted a little longer and at least have heard Romeo speak.

"That was rude," he said to Sheila, referring to her response to Darlene.

"Absolutely, she clearly doesn't have a clue about socializing in this town. How could she just walk up to someone and insult the host like that? And what the heck is a *husboy*?" She laughed. Seeing that Sheila was wound up and a little tipsy, Evan decided to let it go.

As the night went on, they got food from the buffet, where Sheila's Cucumber Lemon Orzo Salad was a big hit. She had cut out red and white radish stars and placed them on top to fit in with the theme. Several women complimented it and asked for the recipe.

Sheila made sure they made the rounds to connect with all of Evan's colleagues and their wives. They talked with Evan's friend Gary about collecting donations for a charity golf tournament in which they were competing later that month. Laura, another law associate at his firm, joined the discussion, and she was also competing in the golf tournament. Laura was tall and striking, with another shorter African American woman next to her. Laura had dark skin and a short-cropped afro and wore a well-tailored masculine pants suit. The conversation went on about the tournament, and Sheila, wanting to find her entry into the conversation, asked Laura who her friend was.

"Oh, I am so sorry, this is Monica, my wife," she paused, "It still sounds funny saying that, but we were married in June after being together for three years. She just packed up our house in Berkeley and moved up here to join me."

"Congratulations!" Gary said, "and welcome to the Rogue Valley. I hear that your wife is an incredible lawyer and a heck of a good golfer as well."

"Monica just started working as a fitness trainer at Snap Fitness" Laura said, "and is also doing a few gigs as a private chef. I benefit by being able to eat outrageously delicious food and stay in shape at the same time." They all laughed.

One of the serving staff interrupted with a request that everyone gathers outside for a brief welcome speech by Roger McSmith. Once everyone crowded around the pool, he thanked them for coming, stated that it had been a very profitable year for the law firm, thanked his wife, and invited everyone to raise their glasses and give three cheers for the U.S.A.

Soon after the sun had set, everyone huddled outside around the massive kidney-shaped pool for a view of the fireworks. Kapow, drizzle, drizzle. Whoosh, tzee, drizzle, drizzle. For over half an hour, ever more fantastic explosions lit up the night sky, synchronized with music over the speaker system from the local radio station. Evan put his arms around an excited Sheila, who kissed him as the finale exploded over the night sky to the sounds of Rossini's William Tell Overture.

"I love you, Evan. Happy Fourth!" Sheila whispered in Evans ear.

"I love you to the moon and back, honey," he replied.

That night, as Evan slept soundly, Sheila let out a gut-wrenching cry. She was in terrible pain, drenched with sweat, and lying in a pool of blood. Evan called an ambulance, which rushed her to the Providence Hospital emergency room. Before she got there, she knew that she had lost a second baby, the one conceived during their trip to India. This time, the doctor said that the complications were such that there could be no more babies from Sheila's womb.

Barb came down and stayed with them for three weeks. Sheila cried when she left, but she was crying most days anyway, curled up on the sofa in a fetal position. The hospital social worker had told Evan not to push her on adoption until she adjusted to the idea that she would not bear a child and offered to arrange mental health counseling for her, or for both of them, when Sheila was ready.

For the next month, he worked from home most days to keep an eye on her and learned to make meals from home-delivered boxed-dinner kits that he bought online. She slowly began to accept the reality that she would never be a mother, at least not to a child that she brought into the world. Her friend Karen came to visit her on Strawberry Lane, coaxed her out of the house for coffee, and eventually convinced her to join her for a low-impact aerobics class at the Medford Y.

Work was getting increasingly tedious and unfulfilling for Evan. He was one of six associates at the firm, each competing for the four managing partners' attention and approval. He had never been an exceptionally bright student, and his specialty in corporate law was more mechanical and rote, depending mostly on paying attention to repetitive details and managing paperwork for small businesses, estates, and non-profits. He relied on Laura a lot for help when he couldn't figure out which codes to apply or statutes to reference. Laura was a rock star at the firm and the only Black, and only female associate.

Laura partnered with Don Paramus, one of the McSmith firm's founding partners, for the Lions Club charity golf tournament. Not only did they raise the highest amount of money, but they also came out on top of the leaderboard and won the coveted trophy for the firm. When combined with all the extra cases she had volunteered to take on, she saw a hefty bonus or a promotion coming soon.

Monica stood in the awards ceremony audience, beaming with pride in the Stoneridge clubhouse where the results were read. She had taken the afternoon off work from the fitness center. After a round of applause for the third and second place winners, the winning McSmith team names were called out, and Don Paramus motioned to his wife to join him and Laura on the stage. As the applause continued, Laura motioned for Monica to come up as well. As she stepped up and the applause died down, the two women noticed a decided reduction in the room's temperature, as broad smiles turned to looks of confusion.

CHAPTER 7

CAMPFIRE AND CANDLEGLOW

An unusually high number of ghosts and goblins visited the Vickerson house on Halloween night of 2019. There were a few princesses and superheroes and even some "Stranger Things" characters who knocked on their door. Sheila went through three bags of candy, and all of the homemade Rice Crispy treat bars. Evan noticed her wistful look when answering the door and worried that she was thinking of how things could have been if she had carried the babies to term.

Evan was up early the next morning getting ready for his weekend trip to Lake of the Woods. Gary, his golfing buddy, had put together a late-season trip up to his cabin and it coincided with Evan's thirty-second birthday. Gary worked as an artistic director at Harry and David's, putting together some of their catalogs and seasonal promotional materials. In addition to Evan, he had invited his younger brother Malcolm, Tez from pinochle game nights, and a new guy named Gregory.

Gary picked up Evan last in his Tahoe Expedition utility wagon, and they drove for about forty miles east of Talent, up the steep twists and turns of Dead Indian Memorial Highway. Evan noticed the last lingering leaves of fall color and thought about how quickly the year had gone by, from vibrant spring in India to the summer tragedy of losing the baby and now moving into the chill and shorter days of fall.

The log cabin was very spacious and modern with a large sunken living room, a full kitchen, two large bedrooms, and a futon sofa in the living room. Evan was assigned to one of the queen beds in a room with the new guy, who would be arriving later. Gary and Malcolm had the other room, and Tez got the futon. They unpacked the supplies and prepared some sandwiches before heading out for a hike around the lake. When they got back, the new guy had arrived and was in the bedroom. Evan went into the bedroom and introduced himself.

"Oh, hi, dude. I just got here. I had a matinee to do this afternoon and it was our last show of the season so that I couldn't get away until now," he said as he flipped off his shoes, "We actually met this summer at that Fourth of July party at your boss's house on the mountain." Evan blushed with embarrassment as he recalled the awkwardness of being dragged away from the couple by Sheila.

"Oh, I'm sorry about that. My wife can be a little brusque at times. She means well."

"That's cool. Darlene can be pretty much 'in your face' as well." In one fluid movement, Gregory removed his sweatshirt and undershirt to reveal a beautifully-chiseled chest, which elicited a subtle reaction from Evan that he quickly suppressed. "I've been needing this all day!" Gregory exclaimed as he ripped off his pants and underwear, tossed them on the bed, and ran out on the deck to jump into the hot tub.

Soon, the other guys joined him in the hot tub in their swimsuits and made introductions. Gary met Gregory during a talk-back session with the actors after one of the performances of Romeo. When he discovered that they were both Carnegie Mellon alums, he struck up a quick friendship and invited him on this trip.

After a quick soak in the hot tub, Gary and Malcolm left the guys and took the boat out to the middle of the lake before it got dark to cast about for dinner. Once they caught about half a dozen brown trout, they headed back to shore. They brought the fish back to the cabin, cleaned them, and then built an open fire on the shore to grill the fish. They doused the fire and crushed the embers thoroughly afterward. After dinner, they played a game of pinochle. Gregory had never played pinochle before and soon became frustrated with all the rules and retreated to their bedroom. After several losing rounds, Evan also decided to call it a night.

"How did you do out there?" Gregory asked.

"The cards weren't in my favor," Evan replied, "Thank goodness we were playing for fun and not playing for money. What are you reading?"

"James Baldwin. Giovanni's Room. Ever read it?" asked Gregory.

"No, but I've read *Go Tell It on the Mountain* and *The Fire Next Time*. He's a brilliant African American writer. I mean 'writer,' he's a brilliant American writer." Evan feared that he might have said something offensive. Gregory smiled and returned to his book. Evan studied Gregory's face, trying not to be caught staring. As he was trying to think of a different topic that would break the ice, his cell phone rang.

It was Sheila calling and he stepped outside to talk privately. It was the first night that they had been apart since she lost the baby. In fact, except for the nights that she was in the hospital, it was the first night apart since she went back to Minnesota for an elderly aunt's funeral five years ago. She just wanted to say goodnight and that she missed him. He told her a little about the day and joked about the "giant" fish that the guys caught. He had worried about leaving her alone, but Barb had said it would be good to give her some space.

He didn't mention Gregory. She told him that she loved him, and he said, "I love you to the moon and back." before he hung up. When he got back to the room, Gregory was fast asleep with the book in his hands, snoring gently. Evan put the book away and pulled the blanket up over him. He slept incredibly soundly and peacefully that night in the stillness and quiet of the cabin.

The next morning was chilly, and the guys were up early for a hearty breakfast and lots of coffee. They went for a strenuous two-hour hike around the lake and up some trails on the side of the mountain. Tez was a birdwatcher and pointed out different species along the way - scrub jays, osprey, pine siskin, and red-bellied woodpeckers. They ended up back at the day tripper's resort's restaurant for lunch. Gary, Malcolm, and Evan went out on the boat to fish for supper while Tez and Gregory rented paddleboats. Later, they all got together in the pool hall to shoot a few rounds of billiards.

Once it got dark, they went out by the lake to look up at the canopy of stars. The sky was clear, and the night sky was full of stars. Malcolm was an astronomy buff and pointed out the North Star, the Little Dipper, and the Big Dipper. He pointed out Orion and led them from there to Gemini and Taurus. He even traced out the stars in Cassiopeia. Later that evening, after dinner, they built a fire in the cabin's big open-hearth fireplace and sipped hot dark chocolate mixed with a hearty dose of Bailey's. Gary talked about a photoshoot he once did in Tahiti with a Sports Illustrated swimsuit model.

"The guys on the crew were all drooling over her knockers, and she was a real cock tease." Evan's mind began to wander as Gary elaborated on his very randy tall tale. His eyes kept darting over to Gregory, drawn into his beautiful green eyes, fine features, square jaw, and skin the color of delicious caramel. He noticed the tattoo on his upper arm of a red heart with a blue rabbit inside it. He wondered what the tattoo meant.

Tez pulled out his guitar and sang a couple of twangy Johnny Cash songs, ending with a heartfelt rendition of Folsom Street Blues. Malcolm was in the corner of the room, aimlessly working on the one-thousand-piece jigsaw puzzle of a beach scene with two Adirondack chairs that he had started that morning.

The lights suddenly shut off and the room went dark. Gary came out of the kitchen with a store-bought chocolate birthday cake ablaze with thirty-two candles. They sang an off-key "Happy Birthday" to Evan, who dutifully blew out the candles. Right before he exhaled, his eyes locked with Gregory and they both smiled. Gary cut big chunks of cake for everyone, which they washed down with more hot chocolate and Baileys.

Gregory asked to borrow Tez's guitar and began singing a romantic ballad called *Loving You*. Evan heard his baritone voice intone the lyrics about love not being a choice and being something that gives purpose to life. They applauded.

"That's pretty nice, man. Never heard that one before," Malcolm said.

"It's a Sondheim song from the musical *Passion*. I performed the lead in Pittsburgh a few years back."

"How did you get into theater?" Malcolm asked.

"Lena Horne," Gregory said with a laugh, "I was always fascinated with Lena Horne. My dad showed me a video of her one-woman show called "The Lady and Her Music." She came out all dolled up and fabulous in glittery costumes and sang Broadway show tunes like *If You Believe* and *The Surry with the Fringe on Top*. And I wanted to <u>be</u> Lena Horne. I wanted to belt out *Stormy Weather*. I saw all of her movies and read her biography. You know, she was supposed to be mulatto Julie in Showboat and sang the role, but MGM cast Ava Gardner in dark make-up instead of her because of discrimination. Hollywood was not ready for a beautiful Black diva like her. I couldn't be her, so I started to sing like her and I was pretty good. I got some excellent roles in high school plays, the lead in *Pippin,* and in *West Side Story*. I was the biggest drama queen in high school. My mom, my brother, and I would drive from D.C. to Manhattan for the weekend just to see *Book of Mormon* or *Aladdin* or *Raisin in the Sun*, pretty much any Broadway show. I did some community theater, which led to a scholarship to study theater at Carnegie Mellon, where I developed a love for the classics, as well as the silly camp stuff. I thought about going to New York or London after college, but I knew that I would get a lot more work to hone my craft in Ashland. I think about Lena each time that I get to go on that stage as a Black man playing Romeo to hundreds of people."

"That's a great story," Evan said. Everyone agreed and busied themselves with clearing up the dishes and cups from the birthday celebration. It was their last night at the cabin, and they started setting up for one last pinochle game. Evan and Gregory said good night and headed off to their room.

Once they were alone in their bedroom, Evan said, "Thanks for that song. It was beautiful." Gregory moved closer and said, "I sang that song for you. Happy Birthday, Evan Vickerson." For the first time in his life, Evan followed an instinct that had no connection to anything he had ever done. He kissed Gregory.

"I have never done anything like this in my life. Kiss a man," Evan said.

"That's OK. I've kissed lots of them," Gregory said as he kissed him again. Before long, they were naked in one of the beds, and Evan was following Gregory's lead. Kissing, touching, caressing, and engaging all those pleasurable places. They could overhear the guys in the other room, laughing and talking. At first, they tried to keep quiet and minimize their noise, but eventually, passion took over, and that effort was abandoned. Gregory let Evan take the lead but slowed things down before he reached a climax.

"This is amazing," Evan said as he rolled over on his back, panting heavily. Gregory smiled and pulled him close, stroking his hair and massaging his temples until he fell asleep.

The next morning, Evan un-entwined himself from Gregory's arms and legs to creep out of bed and put on his running gear. In the living room, the jigsaw puzzle on the side table was ninety percent completed, just a bit of missing sky. He tiptoed through the room, trying not to disturb Tez on the futon bed. He grabbed his light jacket and went out the door and was invigorated by the crisp morning air.

"What had just happened?" he asked himself as he began to pick up his running pace. "Should I tell Sheila?" He had never been unfaithful to her. "Could she handle it with all that has gone on with losing the baby?" He wondered if the urges that surfaced with Gregory just about this one particular person who cast a spell over him or was there something more that connected him to something called a gay community. "Would it happen again?" He looked for some answers in the trees, the sky, and the lake, but he only got more questions.

When he got back from his run, the guys had already started to pack up and clean the cabin. They had one last breakfast together, and no one said a word about what they must have heard from Gregory and Evan's room the night before.

No one was surprised when Evan volunteered to ride back to town in Gregory's old grey two-door Honda Civic. Brightly-colored bumper stickers covered the entire rear side of the car, promoting every progressive cause: *Stop the Jordan Cove Pipeline, Co-exist, Black Lives Matter, Medicare For All, Pro-Choice Voter.*

The guys gave each other quick "bro hugs" all around, promised to get together to do it again soon, and were on their way. As they weaved their way down the mountain, Gregory talked about packing up to go down to Los Angeles for some auditions so that he would have work during the offseason. He was already cast for OSF shows in the spring and not willing to endure winter in southern Oregon. He had friends in Palm Springs and would hang out down there as long as he could.

There was a lot of nervous small talk about the deer roaming the streets in Ashland, why there was a loud train signal whistle for a slow-moving freight train at 4:00 am very morning, how the town of Talent got its unusual name, favorite wineries, and hiking trails. When they arrived at Evan's house, he gathered his things, thanked Gregory for the ride, and reached for the door handle. Gregory reached over and touched Evan's knee. He looked him in the eye and said, "I want to see you again. I really enjoyed last night." Evan smiled and let out a deep breath, relieved to hear this acknowledgment that something special had happened.

"I would like that," he said, got out of the car, and stood on the street grinning ear-to-ear and watching as Gregory drove away.

When he walked into the house, he discovered that Sheila was on the phone with Barb. She covered the mouthpiece and whispered, "It's Eddie. He packed up and left a note saying that he was going to Korea and said something about 'karma.'"

CHAPTER 8

CHESTNUTS ROASTING

Evan looked out of the picture window of the Strawberry Lane house on a cold dreary wintry November day. The drizzle, mixed with the cold misty fog and the last fading yellow rose of the season just outside his window perfectly matched his melancholy mood. It was snowing heavily up in the mountains. He had taken some work home, but couldn't focus on deeds and cost-reimbursable contracts when his mind kept wandering back to that night at Lake of the Woods.

When Sheila came into the den, he suddenly clicked out of his daze and pretended to be working on his laptop. She wanted to review the Christmas card list with him. It wasn't even Thanksgiving yet, but she needed urgently to make sure that all of his business associates and extended family were included. He approved the list and after she left the room, he clicked on the OSF website which still had pictures of his "Romeo" on the front page.

He had seen Gregory a couple of times since the camping weekend before he left for the winter in warmer climates. Each time there was a passionate sexual encounter, followed by intense guilt and confusion. He wasn't sleeping well and couldn't concentrate. It was becoming noticeable at work when he would suddenly hear his name called at staff meetings and had no idea what was being discussed. He was making technical errors that he had never made before.

He needed to talk to someone, but he didn't know anything about same-sex attraction and didn't know anyone who was gay... except for his colleague Laura, who had been so inelegantly outed at the golf tournament. Laura had spent the morning helping him with a tricky tax case for a client and he suggested they take a lunch break. He offered to take her to the Common Block Restaurant, near their Medford office.

"I'm really sorry about what happened to you and your girlfriend at the golf tournament." Evan said after several minutes of talking about work issues.

"Thanks," she said, "I was warned that this area is not as progressive as Berkeley and I guess the sight of a Black lesbian couple was a little more than McSmiths was ready for. You are actually the first person at the firm who has mentioned anything about it since it happened back in July." she said, while he nervously contemplated his grilled salmon and spinach salad.

"Well, actually, I um," he stumbled around for the right words. "I've recently, I mean, this is something new to me. I um."

"You're gay!" she said, hoping to help him get on with it.

"No, no, no. I mean, I'm not sure. I'm married to Sheila and I love her. But I just met this guy and I've never done anything like this in my life, but we met on this camping trip and it just happened."

"You need to be more specific here, Evan. What 'just happened'?" she asked.

"Well, we've been seeing each other. Having sex together. I don't know what you'd call it." Lowering his voice and looking around to make sure no one was within earshot.

"I see," she said. He explained what had happened in the cabin and since then with Gregory.

"So, what do I do now? He's married to a woman too. We've only been together three times, but each time it just gets better and better. I crave his smell, his touch. I can't stop thinking about him. When I'm at work, I go to this website to see pictures of him and be reminded of how gorgeous he is. I've never done anything like this and I'm afraid that I might do something that I will regret. Something that might hurt Sheila."

"Well, it's none of my business, Evan, but I think having a secret affair is already hurting her and hurting you. Before Monica, I almost married a guy who was on the down-low. In his twisted mind, he thought that sleeping around with men was not cheating. When he gave me an STD for the third time, he finally came clean. Not saying that this is the same situation with your guy, but Sheila seems like a nice woman and she could be in for a whole lot of hurt if you don't clue her into what's going on."

"I get that. She means the world to me and I want to be the man that she wants me to be. She wants a family and a white picket fence and a happily ever after. I want that too, but something about being with Gregory just feels so natural. I don't want to lose him and I know that he is feeling the same thing." He immediately regretted that he had revealed his lover's name, but couldn't take it back.

"Then you need to make a choice, Evan. Is this man worth ending your commitment to Sheila? That's what you need to decide for yourself." Evan let that sink in for a minute. The waiter interrupted by asking if they needed anything else and this prompt made them realize that they needed to get back to the office.

"Thanks, Laura. You gave me some things to think about." She promised to keep their conversation confidential and agreed to be available if he wanted to talk more. As they approached their office building, Laura remembered an openly-gay minister that she met at the United Methodist Church. She gave Evan his contact information and suggested that he might be a good person to talk with about his dilemma. Evan took the card and tried to get up the courage to call a couple of times, but always held back at the last minute. It was hard enough having the conversation with someone that he knew, but couldn't imagine sharing this secret with a stranger and definitely not with a clergyman.

As Thanksgiving approached, he convinced himself that what had happened with Gregory was a one-time thing that would never happen again. He wasn't attracted to men, it was just this one crazy birthday weekend that had been taken way out of proportion. He loved Sheila and the life they had together, even though it wasn't perfect. If he would just focus more on her, then this "thing" would go away.

Thanksgiving weekend was all about Sheila. On Thanksgiving Day, Evan took his wife out to a prix-fixe holiday feast at Lark's, a gourmet, four-star hotel restaurant in the center of downtown Ashland. He had to pull some strings to get a reservation at the last minute. The day after Thanksgiving, they went to the Festival of Light evening parade in Ashland. Sheila loved parades and this annual parade celebrated all the winter holiday traditions and ended with the arrival of Santa and Mrs. Claus, who flipped the switch that turned on holiday lights throughout the whole downtown. That weekend they drove to Bend to ski at the Mt. Bachelor resort with Gary and his wife. After a day of skiing, they built a big fire in the hotel room fireplace to roast chestnuts and melt smores. They played a round of Charades and snuggled up listening to Johnny Mathis music.

Gregory called during the week after Thanksgiving. Evan ignored the call and erased the voicemail message without listening to it. He was getting his life back on track and giving all of his attention to his marriage and his job. A week later Gregory called again and this time, without thinking about it, he answered. He was in Palm Springs and Evan could hear splashing about in the swimming pool in the background. Evan fought the feeling of happiness he felt on hearing his voice again. He could tell from his slurred diction that he had had more than a few early afternoon cocktails.

"Hey Evan, man, I really miss you. What's been cooking up your way?"

"Nothing special," Evan said, "Just work and trying to get into the holiday spirit."

"Well ho, ho, ho. It's always a holiday down here." He told Evan about the two commercials that he shot in L.A., his audition for an episode of Law and Order SVU, and the clothing-optional resort where he was spending the weekend. "Wish you could hop down here, dude."

"Yes, I'm sure that would be nice," Evan said. There was a click on his phone indicating an incoming text. He opened it to a selfie picture of Gregory's beautifully bronzed naked body lying in a lounge chair. Before he knew it, Evan was using the video call function to have his first phone sex experience.

"Well, I gotta go, Evan," Gregory said after they finished. "Thanks for indulging me. I really do miss our time together. You have no idea how hot you are. Rehearsals start in late January for the next season at OSF, so we'll be back up there next month. See you then, OK?"

"O.K.," Evan said and hung up. He immediately started to fight back the guilt, rationalizing that just having phone sex was not cheating on Sheila. No worse really than a guy watching porn. There was no emotional commitment there and maybe it would improve their sex life if he had some of these newly-discovered fantasies fulfilled. Perhaps when she was more stable, they could talk about it and figure out a way that he could explore this expanding range of his sex life.

Evan and Sheila spent Christmas in Tigard with Evan's parents, as they usually did. Barb made sure that they had the Norman Rockwell picture-perfect Christmas dinner, with a perfectly browned twenty-pound turkey and all the fixings. Sheila made Mary Berry's Partridge in a Pear Tart dessert that she had seen demonstrated on the *Great British Baking Show*.

The table seemed empty without Eddie there loading up his plate. A cheap religious Christmas card was the only communication from him over the past two months. Inside, it simply said, "Mom and Dad. Arrived OK in Seoul. Don't worry.

Eddie." Of course, Barb worried all the time about him, especially whether he was maintaining his sobriety.

After dinner, they gathered around the big over-decorated Christmas tree to open gifts – hand-knitted scarfs for everyone from Barb, a Harry and David holiday basket from Evan and Sheila to his parents, a Brookstone heated foot massager from Jerry to Barb, gold earrings and a bracelet from Evan to Sheila, and a large gold foil-wrapped mystery box from Sheila to Evan. It was unusually light in weight for the size, so Evan shook it.

"Let's hope it's not a glass figurine," Barb said, and they all laughed. Once he tore off the wrapping and unsealed the box, he felt through the tissue paper to discover a small envelope that held two V.I.P. tickets to the New Year's Eve performance by Pink Martini in Schnitzer Hall.

"Thanks, honey. That's so sweet of you." He shared with his parents that they had seen the band Pink Martini in Corvallis on their first solo date.

On New Year's Eve, Sheila came into the living room dressed in a sleek form-fitting black dress with glimmering scarlet red beading around the collar and the earrings and bracelet that Evan gave her for Christmas. Evan appeared in a smart black suit with a black silk shirt and a bright red bow tie to match Sheila. Barb snapped some pictures as though they were going to first prom together.

Once at the theater, the usher seated them in the second row of the orchestra in the sold-out concert hall. Instruments for the twenty-piece band were pre-set on the stage, and the crowd went wild when Thomas Lauderdale and the band came out and took their places. As the last song before the intermission, China Forbes invited women to come on stage to join in singing Helen Reddy's *I am Woman.*

Sheila was right up front among about a hundred women who heeded the call. Evan clapped and sang along, cheering and snapping pictures on his cellphone. He tried to banish thoughts of Gregory and congratulated himself that he had successfully resisted the frequent urge to call him in southern California over the holidays, especially tonight.

The concert ended at about 11:15 pm with an extended standing ovation and a conga line through the concert hall during the encore. As part of their V.I.P. package, Sheila and Evan got to stay in the hall for drinks, hors d'oeuvres, and dancing. As it got close to midnight, some band members came back out to play Auld Lang Syne to an afro-Cuban beat, led by one of the soloists. Like most of the couples in the hall, Evan and Sheila kissed after the midnight countdown.

Evan said, "Thank you for the concert, honey. What a perfect way to end the year!" and Sheila replied, "I have a feeling that 2020 is going to be an incredibly wonderful year."

CHAPTER 9

THE NEW NORMAL?

Along with the first tiniest blossoms of spring came the horrible pandemic, when a virus closed everything down and faces retreated, hidden behind cloth masks or plastic shields. Evan had to work mostly from home, sequestered in the den. Sheila knew that area was off-limits, and he was always on video conference calls anyway.

Staying home all day was maddening for Sheila. Cook, clean, read books, watch tragic news on television, talk with Barb on the phone, repeat. She had always loved retail therapy at Rogue Valley Mall, but the stores were all closed, and online shopping just didn't have the same thrill. She couldn't go to the gym to workout with Karen or the library for her weekly Scrabble group meeting. So, she cooked and ate what she cooked, which gained her the dreaded "COVID Fifteen" pounds.

On the first official day of spring, she planted some new yellow rose bushes next to the picket fence around their house, which she hand-painted a glossy white enamel. She took a nightly walk just around sunset and sometimes coaxed Evan to come along. As soon as he got back, he would go straight back to the office and often work until late at night. Their sex life was occasional and mechanical.

Gregory returned from southern California in late January and eagerly threw himself into daily rehearsals for the next play. He also made time for a weekly rendezvous with Evan. They usually met at Gregory's apartment for a little conversation and a lot of sex. Much of that conversation was about the play and backstage machinations that Evan didn't understand. Through the first months of 2020, Evan often told Sheila that he had to meet a client or do some library research at the office in the middle of the day. That's when he met Gregory at his townhouse for an hour or so of pure, unbridled pleasure.

In March, Gregory learned that, like so many others, he was furloughed due to the pandemic and lockdown orders. They were just a week into performances of "Peter and the Starcatcher" and suddenly he was home with nothing to do. He was at the pinnacle of his career, but now uncertain whether his chosen career would ever provide opportunities to work again any time soon.

Just a few weeks of quarantine had Gregory climbing the walls, so he invited Evan to join him for a walk along the Ashland Railroad Park. It had rained on that early spring morning, but the sun came out for them and the air was fresh and clear. The paved park trail extended for about a mile and a half paralleling the railroad tracks from the old downtown train depot to a cemetery on the outskirts of town.

Evan had never been to this park and he marveled at all the artwork along the trail. He also admired his friend's perceptions of all the little things that he would never have noticed, like the flocks of starling birds sweeping from the ground up into the trees. They stopped along the trail to admire elaborate sculptures made of colorful reclaimed broken cups and bottles, a chain link fence filled with hundreds of brightly colored combination locks, an alpaca grazing on a farm across the railroad track. At the cemetery, they read the headstones and made up elaborate stories about who these people were. They sat on a bench to eat some sandwiches that Gregory brought along and watch joggers, walkers, and bikers pass by.

"How did you and Darlene meet?" Evan asked.

"We met during our senior year at Carnegie Mellon. We were both in the Drama School and she got kicked out of student housing and moved into the group house that I shared with some other students. We connected right away when we learned that we were both polyamorous. Do you know what that means?" he asked. When Evan shook his head, he answered, "We are each attracted to both genders and are open to sexual experiences with men and women. It's totally liberating and expands your sexual and emotional repertoire in amazing ways. We even slept with some of the same people, but never at the same time." He paused for a reaction from Evan. When there was none, he continued, "It's kind of funny how we got married. I was offered an eight-month contract to join the OSF professional company and there was also the possibility of a job for Darlene in the costume department. On Halloween, we smoked a lot of pot, went to City Hall with some friends, and got married dressed as Frankenstein and the Bride of Frankenstein. We celebrated by getting matching tattoos of a rabbit holding a pumpkin inside the outline of a heart, the rabbit symbolizing fertility and speed, the pumpkin reminding us of Halloween and the heart representing our love for each other. That was two years ago."

"That is so crazy, and just a little romantic too," Evan said, gently touching his tattoo.

"A couple of weeks after we were married, we packed up a U-Haul and headed west for our new adventure. We stopped in Kentucky to see her crazy family. Then, we stopped in Denver and went to the Red Rocks Amphitheater when it was completely empty and we jumped on stage and belted out "Rocky Mountain High" at the top of our lungs. We drove all night and got here just as the sun was rising over Grizzly Peak. We both really love southern Oregon, and the counter-culture community of people here in the valley, who are open to a lifestyle of gender fluidity and sexual freedom. But we always tell each other when we mess around with someone outside the marriage. As Darlene always says 'lack of communication and secrets are like kryptonite to a happy marriage.'"

What Gregory failed to say though, was that, for the first time since he met Darlene, he felt compelled to keep a secret. He hadn't told her about his relationship with Evan. He wasn't exactly sure why he kept this relationship to himself. There was something different about this man. With the pandemic restrictions, he was being careful not to sleep around with other guys and made and kept that commitment to Evan.

They continued to meet on and off through the spring and into the summer. Evan took every chance he could, and a few risks, to be with Gregory. It was soon apparent that Gregory loved nothing more than talking about himself and he had some great stories. He was ambitious, self-confident and a man in a hurry to grab for everything he could in life. But this over summer he was reduced to taking a part-time job as a clerk in the tasting room of a local winery to help make ends meet. He cringed when he was recognized by customers who had seen him on stage, but put on a smile and cheery attitude to sell more wine.

There was no Independence Day parade in the year of the pandemic. Evan grilled some baby back ribs in the backyard and Sheila baked a cherry/apple pie. That afternoon, they assembled with their amply-filled plates at the dining table and rolled in the big-screen television for a Zoom holiday family dinner party with Barb and Jerry, Jerry's widowed mother in Hood River, and an assortment of Barb's brothers, cousins, nephews and nieces. During the meal, there was a round-robin of updates from each of the squares on the screen. On their turn, Sheila just said that they were "holding down the fort in Talent." After they signed off, they returned to a familiar pattern. Sheila cleared the dishes and watched an episode of "The Crown" and Evan did some work in the den.

In late July, Evan took Gregory on an overnight trip to Gold Beach on the Oregon Coast. He told Sheila that one of their clients had a business that was going bankrupt there and that he had to be on-site to review some of their books and documents. It was just overnight, but it was the first chance that they had to spend a night together since Lake of the Woods. They took the scenic three-hour drive through the mountains and the redwoods and up the rugged coastline to reach the small beachfront town. They checked into a motel room with a balcony overlooking the Pacific Ocean.

Gregory quickly slipped on a swimsuit and ran down the path to the sandy beach and into the cold, raging ocean water. Evan caught up but didn't go beyond the shoreline. When Gregory came ashore and dried off, they walked along the sandy beach holding hands, frolicking, and collecting seashells. Evan couldn't remember a time that he felt such freedom and joy. When the wind picked up, they returned to the room, took a long sensual shower together, put on the hotel-issued terrycloth bathrobes, and went out on the balcony with a bottle of expensive Pinot Gris from the winery where Gregory worked.

"So, what's the first thing that you are going to do when this pandemic is over?" Evan asked after a few glasses of the wine.

"I'm going to go to the middle of Lincoln Center in New York City right in front of the fountain," he said, "and I'm going to hug random strangers. Big juicy, never-letting-you-go-again hugs. I'm going to kiss all the men and women on their lips – all of them - old, young, rich, poor, pretty, ugly. Just memorize every face that I can see and give big sloppy kisses with no masks on, no distance between us. I'm going to yell 'Fuck Social Distancing! Fuck the virus! We are all free!'" When their laughter finished, Gregory returned the question to Evan.

"I think if this were over I would quit my job, find a way to leave Sheila and come back to this beach and just spend a lot of days and nights with you."

"Here's to that," Gregory said and raised his wine glass. They kissed and then looked out at the orange-tinted sun that was just beginning to kiss the horizon.

Back in Medford, Sheila was hurrying to get to her Zumba class at the Medford Y. The gyms were still open and one of the few places to gather publicly, though with strict safety protocols and by appointment only. She passed a pretty little girl sitting quietly with a coloring book just outside the door to the workout room.

Carolina, the Zumba instructor, took the eight women and one man through an energetic hour-long routine that left everyone sweaty and energized. Evan's secretary Marlene was in the class and Sheila went over to her afterwards and made small talk about his business trip to see a client in Gold Beach. Marlene had no idea what Sheila was talking about, but had enough experience with unfaithful male bosses that she went along with the ruse.

After the class, Sheila asked Carolina and Linda, her eight-year-old daughter, to join her for lunch at the organic café next door to the Y thank her for the class. Once they were seated in the café, Sheila asked, "Do you and your husband have other children?"

"I have another daughter who is thirteen. My husband is in Guadalajara with our teenage son, Julio," she said, struggling a bit with English, "Diego came to Medford ten years ago to work in the pear orchards and he would come every year. Two years ago, he brought me and the kids here and we saved up to buy a small house for all of us to be together. I started teaching dance classes and the kids were doing great in school, learning English and making friends. Then *l'emigra* came last winter after the harvest and deported him. I did not want him to be alone, so Julio went back to be with him. They will try to come back next summer."

"It must be very difficult for you. Are the girls still in school?" She looked over at Linda's big brown eyes, approving and admiring her crayon work. "Linda looks like she wants to be an artist someday."

"Yes, Linda is in second grade and she always drawing and making art. Her sister Flora is the really smart one. She is starting Algebra already at school and the teachers, they all say she is so smart. But I worry that the other students in the class are way behind and don't challenge her. Now that classes are all by computer she says that it is so hard for her.   The school gave us a laptop, but it does not work a lot of the time."

"I used to love math at school," Sheila said. "Perhaps I can help." They talked as they ate their lunch about the some of the horrors that Carolina's family endured getting across the border. Hearing her family saga made Sheila feel incredibly grateful for the material things that she had and realized that during such stressful times, it would help her to focus on other people.

She volunteered to tutor Flora and had a spare desktop computer that she would give to her. She kept watching Linda at the dinner table as she made progress with her drawings. After she paid the check and they were ready to leave, Linda tore the page she was working on out of her coloring book and gave it to Sheila. It showed a mother and daughter in raincoats and umbrellas; the mother was holding her daughter's hand to cross the street.

When Sheila got home, she was eager to call Evan at the beach and tell him all about running into Marlene at the Zumba class and about her new friend Carolina. As she entered the door, she discovered that Mr. Peeps had vomited again on the sofa and was in a corner wheezing and having labored breathing. He was fourteen years old and had gotten several infections that year. She took him to the emergency animal clinic and spent four hours there while they pumped him with antibiotics and medications and watched his recovery before she could take him home. She called Evan from the pet hospital and left a detailed message, since he didn't pick up.

Evan returned home the next morning feeling equal parts elation and guilt. He was having so much fun with Gregory that he had not listened to his phone messages and was unaware that Mr. Peeps had been sick. He lied and said that his phone battery had died and lavished attention on the house pet. He was relieved that they could focus immediate attention on the cat's health and Carolina's family and that he did not have to fabricate an elaborate tale about his "business" in Gold Beach.

A few days later, Flora came to the Medford Y during her mother's class and Sheila took her to the organic café afterwards to work on some practice math problems. She agreed with Carolina that the girl had great academic potential and fell comfortably into her new role as a tutor. She drove Flora home after the session to a well-kept duplex in a lower middle-class neighborhood of West Medford.

Over the next few weeks they developed a routine of meeting at the Y twice a week after exercise class and then going to the café or to Sheila's house for tutoring. The mother/daughter drawing that Linda gave Sheila at the café was prominently displayed on the refrigerator door.

As Sheila's attitude was becoming more positive, she noticed something different in her love life with Evan. After the Gold Beach trip, he was more attentive to her needs in bed. She had never focused much on her own orgasm and suddenly Evan was intent on pleasuring her and spent more time cuddling afterwards. She would often fall asleep with his arms snuggled tightly around her. She was beginning to gain confidence that there was hope for their fragile marriage and that the hard part was behind them. Seeing Flora and Linda a couple of times per week made her think about motherhood again. Mr. Peeps ailing health also worried her about having an empty nest.

On their date night at the Grotto in late August she brought up the subject of adoption for the first time since she lost the second baby last year. She had done research on adoption in Jackson County and brought along brochures about the process and costs that she eagerly shared with Evan.

"Perhaps we should wait until the pandemic is over, honey," he said.

"But that's just the point, this is a perfect time to get things rolling and it's a process that can take months or years. Most people are not thinking about the long term right now. There could even be kids out there who have lost parents to the virus," she said.

"It's not the right time with work and everything," he said, "McSmith's is struggling to get and keep clients and there has been some talk of layoffs and downsizing."

"We have plenty of money left from my inheritance. But, you know, there is another possibility that we might consider," she persisted, "my friend Carolina might be willing to be a surrogate for us. She has had three healthy children and her family could use the money. I asked her about it and she said that she would discuss it with her husband in Mexico. There is no telling when he will be back and she knows other women who have done it for American families. It's a simple medical procedure and, of course, we would cover the delivery cost and legal issues."

"I don't know, honey, it seems like we would be using our white privilege to exploit someone else's misery." Before she could prepare another argument, he said, "This is a lot to take in. Let me give it some thought. I promise that we can talk more about it later." He could tell by her enthusiasm that she was all in on doing this and unlikely to be deterred in her pursuit of enlarging their family unit.

On that fateful afternoon in early September, the day before the Almeda wildfire, Evan sent a text to Gregory saying that he wanted to come over. The office was technically closed for Labor Day Monday, but he spent a few hours on some contract work and made an excuse to Sheila to get out of the house for a couple of hours. Gregory texted back that the coast was clear since Darlene was doing her volunteer work at the La Clinica women's shelter. Evan cranked the volume up on *Blinding Lights* by The Weeknd on his car sound system and drove just above the speed limit as he made the short trip to Gregory's house.

As soon as the door opened, Evan leaped into Gregory's arms and clothes flew in every direction, as they were on to the first round of passionate lovemaking. Afterward, they lay on the floor together, Evan floating in blissful afterglow as he traced the contours of Gregory's perfectly-sculpted face, stroking his wavy hair.

"I'm going to tell Sheila tomorrow," he said, "I can't go on living a lie and now she is talking about adoption. I can't go through the paces with her, when I can only think of being with you. I love you." Gregory knew that he should respond to Evan's daring profession, the first time he had said those words, but instead just pulled him closer to him and kissed him deeply, climbed on top of him to begin another round of intense lovemaking.

CHAPTER 10

RAIN AFTER THE FIRE

Four months had passed since the Almeda fire and four months since Gregory had last spoken with Evan on that cloudless September morning when his heart was broken and his marriage ended. Four months since Sheila tossed her wedding ring into the ash heap of Strawberry Lane. It was a new year now, but the dense fog of tragedy still lingered in the air, just as it had in 2020.

Gregory was recuperating from his car accident in the Talent townhouse that was miraculously spared by the inferno dubbed the Almeda wildfire. High winds and dry conditions set off a spark that flash-destroyed over six hundred homes in a matter of hours in Talent and Phoenix. People were beginning to move around again among the skeletal remains of what used to be modest suburban homes and the landscape was dotted with backhoe equipment and earth movers. There was an odd hodgepodge of intact buildings like City Hall, the high school, the community theater, and Gregory's townhouse community that stood right next to what was once a tree-lined community of trailer and manufactured homes that now looked like the aftermath of nuclear war.

76

Signs all over town read "Talent Strong" and "We'll Get Through This Together." The towns were ever-so-slowly starting to recuperate, rebuilding homes and planting new trees. The FEMA trucks and insurance agents were leaving, and the temporary shelters and food and clothing distribution centers were closed. Coronavirus infections were finally starting to decline, and a few were talking about getting the vaccine. There were even rumors that live theater would be back next summer.

Gregory suffered multiple contusions, fractures, and minor burns from a car accident on the day of the fire. Evan called that morning to tell him that he had come out to Sheila and wanted them to be together, to figure out a way to live together. Gregory rushed over to clear things up and they ended up arguing. Then the emergency alert sounded and as he sped away from the Strawberry Lane house toward safer ground. He swerved to avoid hitting a family of urban deer crossing the street and drove over an embankment and into a creek, banging his head on the steering wheel. When he regained consciousness, trees all around him were ablaze, and he was trapped inside the car. Fortunately, a helicopter spotted him in the blaze, and firefighters rescued him.

Gregory cried out as he relived this in an all too vivid dream. Darlene, lying next to him, shook him awake and reminded him that he was just having a nightmare again. Once he calmed down, she got up, showered, and dressed for work.

"Good morning, husboy." she said, "I left your breakfast on the counter. I will pick up your prescriptions from the pharmacy this afternoon. Jarrod will be here at 4:00 pm for your physical therapy session. After work, I am meeting the girls at Wellsprings. Your lunch is in the fridge, and I will be back in time for dinner. Call if you need anything. Love ya." She kissed him on the forehead and headed out the door to her part-time job at the Ashland Food Coop.

Since he left the hospital, Darlene had been the maestro of his existence, coordinating medical appointments, outpatient surgeries, and she even learned how to give injections and change dressings. He said that she was a combination of nurse Florence Nightingale and impresario Florenz Ziegfield. She deposited his unemployment checks and made sure all the bills were paid. In her spare time, she used her costume-making skills to sew colorful face masks that she sold over the internet. She was his connection to the outside world and his emotional support system for dealing with unemployment and isolation.

Darlene's own emotional support system was the group who called themselves the Wild Girls, consisting of the four B.F.F.s: Glo, Sugar, Monica, and her. Before the pandemic, they had been meeting every Monday night to swim and soak in the therapeutic waters of Jackson Wellsprings on women's night. It had recently re-opened, and they swam, sipped herbal tea, drank Chardonnay, and soaked in the spa. It was their chance to unwind and catch up with each other. As soon as they settled in the huge outdoor hot tub, Monica was first off with some news that shocked the group.

"Laura and I are moving to Seattle," Monica told the girls, "McSmith just promoted two associates to partner and, of course, she wasn't one of them. Two years slaving at that firm, outperforming all of her male colleagues, playing all their political bullshit. She saw the writing on the wall and took a job with a progressive firm in Seattle. We're moving at the end of the month."

"Those fuckers," said Darlene, "Can't she sue them for discrimination?" They all lamented its injustice and how difficult it was for women to be heard and recognized, even when she played by the rules that good old boys set up.

"Turns out, it's not so easy to sue a law firm. It takes years, lots of money and it destroys your ability to get another legal job. Better to just cut your losses and move on," Monica said.

They moved inside to the dry sauna where Darlene reflected on how guilty she felt that she was so happy in a world where there is so much misery. "Gregory is getting stronger every day. I'm busier than ever, but I feel like I am navigating this complicated world of masks and distancing. I think this pandemic has forced us all to slow down and take stock of what's really important. For me, that's our partnership."

"And it probably don't hurt that he can't be catting around while he's in bed recuperating." The girls laughed in agreement with Glo's observation.

"There is more to life than just sex, Glo. Gregory is my soul-mate, my partner in crime. We 'complete each other' in ways that I would never have imagined. I know that you and Laura have the same thing." Darlene said, referring to Monica's wife. "He has his flaws, and so do I, but there is no one that I would rather be with. He's going to come back from the accident and the pandemic, and someday, the world is going to see how incredibly talented he is. How beautiful he is inside. I want that for him."

"I hear you, girl. We got your back, but if he messes with you, we got his back too…with a butcher knife right in the <u>middle</u> of his back," said Sugar, and the girls all laughed in agreement. The hot, dry, eucalyptus-infused air mixed with the Chardonnay was having its desired effects.

"Sorry, but I can't be like that," Darlene insisted, "My happiness cannot be based on some draconian fairy-tale idea of monogamy. We have to both be free to choose, or it doesn't work. I know that I can't be everything for him. He has desires that I can't fulfill, and you girls know that there are times that I need a woman's touch." During their conversation, Sheila's friend Karen had quietly entered the sauna and sat on the lower bench.

"How 'bout you, sistah?" Sugar asked the new person, "Would you be comfortable with your man sleeping with other women…. or men?" Karen felt out of place and explained that she was divorced from a violent husband who had abused her, and she wasn't dating. The Wild Girls leaned in close as she talked about how awful his alcoholism became and how she made some difficult choice to save her life.

The Wild Girls said goodbye to their new friend and gave her hugs and words of encouragement. They took one last dip in the thermal pool and headed to the locker room to get dressed. They hugged and said farewells to Monica as they drove away from Jackson Wellsprings in their separate directions.

Meanwhile, Gregory was lying naked on a massage table, being kneaded and stretched by the strong hands of a Nordic-looking former football player who had found his calling in physical therapy after graduating from SOU. He directed his energy to all those places that needed to be put back into place and a few more special ones that Gregory had grown accustomed to at the end of the formal massage session.

"You are the best," Gregory said, as Jarrod was gently cleaning up, "you should have those hands insured for a million dollars, like a virtuoso violinist."

"Thanks, Mr. Mitchell. It's always a pleasure to work with you. Most of my clients are old and saggy guys, not young and firm like you. You know, I didn't mention this before, but I saw you in Romeo three times. Our senior class went, and I had to write a paper on it. I thought you were fantastic." He started quoting lines from the play in an overly dramatic manner.

"Listen, Jarrod, my wife is going to be home pretty soon, so we better wind things up here. Same time next week?" Gregory said.

"Sure. I'll be out of here in a jiff," Jarrod said as he packed his things up to leave, "Parting 'tis such sweet sorrow." He laughed as Gregory handed him a twenty-dollar bill as a tip. Just then, Gregory's cell phone rang somewhere under the heap of clothes on the bed. Jarrod found the phone and handed it to Gregory, who waited to speak until he was out the door.

"Hello Gregory, it's Evan," said the nervous voice on the other end, "How have you been?"

"A little banged up, but I guess, as Gloria Gaynor would say, 'I will survive.'" He wanted to lighten the mood, but there was more silence, as if neither knew quite what to say next.

Evan broke the silence. "So, it's been a while since I saw you and quite a bit has happened. Sheila left me after the fire. I don't blame her. She took most of the insurance money, accepted a tech job with a company in Portland. She is living with my parents while she waits on the divorce to be final. Mr. Peeps died soon after the fire. I have been staying in a hotel in Ashland." There was a long silence. "I spoke to your wife right after the accident."

"I know. I'm sorry that I haven't been in touch, but I thought it was for the best," Gregory said. There was another silence. "I don't have very much to offer you right now. You're a really good person, Evan, you truly are. I just...."

Evan cut him off. "I know, Gregory, I think I've always known. You take care." He hung up.

Gregory was going over that conversation in his mind when he heard a key in the door, and Darlene came bouncing in with bags of groceries and a rattling key chain. Had he done the right thing? Had he been gentle enough? Did he let Evan know how much their short time together had meant to him?

Darlene had smoked a little pot at the sauna and brought some cannabis edibles to share with Gregory after the take-out dinner from the Ashland Food Co-Op's hot buffet. They tried watching an episode of *Tiger King* on Netflix, but they got a serious case of the giggles and then the drowsies. They fell asleep snuggled in each other's arms.

CHAPTER 11

WINTER WINDS BLOW

Evan had been staying for the past six months since the fire in temporary quarters at the Stratford Inn in Ashland, in a nice enough hotel suite that could seriously use an update. Months of therapy helped him to get in touch with his sexuality and to begin to understand his relationships with Sheila, his parents, and Gregory. He was finally taking some of the advice he had given Eddie about shaping his own destiny.

To his surprise, he had become friends with Gregory and Darlene. They met a couple of times for the Wednesday night ten buck wine dinners at Paschal Winery. Once Gregory got busy with his voice-over and audiobook reading jobs, Darlene focused her attention on Evan and she became his closest confidant. They would get together for a happy hour at a bar or smoke a joint together and talk and laugh for hours. He loved her free spirit and willingness to speak so frankly about sex, something he had never done with Sheila, nor with Gregory. She talked about positions and sex toys in the way that a jock would talk about football plays, she knew all the moves and how to stay ahead in the game.

He felt drained after his online therapy session. He thought of calling Darlene but remembered that she had gone home to visit her family in Louisville.   He decided that taking a walk down to the Black Sheep Pub Restaurant for some hearty Shephard's Pie and a Guinness on a cold winter night in front of the roaring fireplace would be just the right tonic for his mood. He bundled up and put his face mask on.

As he walked down Main Street, he noticed the Happy New Year 2021 banners still hanging from street poles a month after the celebration. The Bloomsbury Bookstore window had "Black Lives Matter" posters up and photo ads of tell-all books about Trump next to Valentine's Day cards. Patrons streamed out of the Varsity Theater from some new horror film that had Oscar buzz. Pre-teens were crowded into Martoli's Pizza, washing down cheese slices with root beer.

He climbed up the long narrow stairs to the Black Sheep's second-floor dining room, where he was seated by a perky waitress. Once seated, he noticed a woman sitting with a young lady behind the plexiglass screen at the table next to him. After ordering his food, he sat with his pint mug of Guinness and kept trying to figure out how he knew her, and the young lady was even more familiar. They were paying their check and about to leave, and Evan had to get their attention.

"Excuse me, but have we met before? You both seem so familiar. My name is Evan."

"Yes, Evan, we have met before. I am Sheila's friend, Karen Zapolski. It's just terrible what you have put that poor lovely girl through. Shame on you." The waiter interrupted with their change, and as they stood up to leave, Evan looked again at the young lady and had another question for Karen.

"Sorry to bother you again, but do you happen to know my parents, Jerry and Barb Vickerson?" Karen's face went pale, and she instinctively grabbed Jennifer's hand and pulled her closer.

"No, I don't believe that I do. Goodbye, Evan," she said with finality and scurried away. Puzzling, but he imagined that Sheila must have talked about his parents, who were now his surrogate parents, with such a good friend.

Evan's food arrived, and he suddenly felt very lonely, eating alone in the cozy restaurant. Sheila had continued to refuse his phone calls and only relayed messages through Barb. Barb and Jerry were confused, embarrassed and angry. At Darlene's suggestion, he sent them a copy of the book "Loving Someone Gay" by Donald Clark, asked them to read it and discuss it with him when they were ready.

He never heard from Gary, Malcolm, and Tez, even for pinochle nights, which they had stopped due to the pandemic.

Things had been awkward with them since the Lake of the Woods trip, and he had to admit that once he started seeing Gregory, he had neglected other friendships. He tried to make some new connections through the men's support group that Darlene recommended, many of them married guys who were bisexual or coming out as gay. It was facilitated by Reverend William from the United Methodist Church, the guy that Laura recommended over a year ago, before he had made such a mess of things. The sessions helped him get to a better understanding of his sexuality and how other men dealt with coming out, but once the meetings at the library conference room were over, everyone scattered.

His firm had suffered a hit from the pandemic and, a couple of months back, they had to lay off most of the associates, including him. He thought about looking for another legal job, but his heart wasn't in it. Sheila had gotten most of the insurance money since the house was in her name, but McSmiths had given him a generous severance that would get him through for a while. He missed the house on Strawberry Lane as he fingered the wedding band that he could not bring himself to remove. He moved the peas around the mashed potatoes in the Shephards Pie. Nothing felt quite right in his life, and he remembered the question that Eddie had asked him all those months ago, "What does it feel like to be normal?"

When Evan got back to the hotel, the young man at the desk told him that he had a package. Once back in his room, he opened the brown bubble-wrap envelope and found a cell phone inside. The police had contacted him a few days earlier and told him that someone found a cell phone when they were demolishing his Strawberry Lane house's remains. They traced it back to him. It was his business phone, and, it had miraculously survived intact.

He started listening to voice messages, which were mostly routine until he heard this one that came in on the September 8th at 2:25 pm, the day of the Almeda fire. "Hello, Mr. Vickerson, my name is John Paolo Stinson, and I am calling on behalf of my mother, Wanda Sambocar. She says that you two met in India last year and she had your business card. She was arrested last night when she returned from New Zealand, for grand theft and said that you would know her story. She needs legal assistance. Please call me back at your earliest convenience at this number."

His first thought was, "Wanda has a son?" He didn't believe she ever mentioned an adult son. And why would she be calling him out of the blue after over a year? He remembered asking her what she would do if the key to the doctors' mansion didn't work and imagined that she must have finally been caught. But surely, she knew that he practiced civil law and not criminal law.

Early the next morning, he called John Paolo's number and learned that Wanda's case was going to court later that month. Her son had retained a local legal team to represent her, but his mother was still asking about Evan. She heard about the fires and would be happy to hear that he and his wife were O.K.

"We're O.K.," he told John Paolo, "but my wife and I are now separated, divorcing. It's a long story."

"Sorry to hear that, Mr. Vickerson," John Paolo said, "I know that you must be very busy, but I am sure that my mother would appreciate it greatly if you could come to her trial for moral support. She doesn't have many friends, well none actually. I would be happy to pay for your travel expenses." It was an odd request, but he wasn't working, and Miami sounded awfully good when it was thirty degrees outside with light snow just beginning to fall.

He wasn't sure why, but he called back the next day to accept John Paolo's offer. Maybe it was because of the confirmation that his curiosity about Wanda's fantastic life story was justified. The trial could fill in more of the blanks about her life. Maybe there was something in John Paolo's voice that made him want to meet this man.

Two weeks later he passed through TSA Pre-Check at the regional airport in Medford on his way to the gate to board flights that would get him to Miami. He didn't notice a trim, well-dressed Asian man coming in on a flight from Los Angeles. Eddie had returned to the U.S. after a long journey of self-discovery in Seoul.

When Eddie arrived in Seoul in November of 2019, he was immediately fascinated with the youthful vibrancy of this modern metropolis of almost ten million people. He stayed with Mochi, his Korean internet pen pal, in his one-bedroom apartment in a renovated factory building in an older section of Seoul. They shared a love of fast-paced video games and would spend hours playing them or watching e-sport stadium gaming competitions, following gamers like professional athletes.

For the first time in his life, he was in a place where everyone looked like him. He didn't have to worry about fitting or not fitting some stereotype or explaining why his parents were white. He quickly made friends who didn't mock him as the nerdy, chubby guy, and he even gained the self-confidence to date a girl. He found a good 12-Step program to help maintain his sobriety and started exercising regularly at a 24-hour gym in their neighborhood.

He met Eunji at a Boba tea shop in the trendy Millae-dong district of Seoul. Eddie and Mochi were using the café's free wi-fi to work on Eddie's resume. Over his laptop screen, he noticed a group of four girls sipping tea, talking and giggling self-consciously while looking in his direction. Eventually, one of the girls came over and said some words in Korean that Mochi translated to Eddie as "My friend thinks you are very cute. Says you look like G-Dragon," the stage name of Kwon Ji Yong, one of the most popular K-pop stars in Korea.

"Tell her that she can only find out if she comes over and joins us," Mochi said in Korean. The girls did so, and Eddie and Eunji dominated the conversation, while the others looked on in admiration. They were fascinated that he was American and peppered him with questions about social media, portion sizes, tipping, and family relationships. Lots of questions about the Kardashians. Each time they laughed at his answers, his eyes darted over to Eunji.

At that very moment, a tour bus was traveling through the streets of Seoul. A tour guide was pointing out the fourteenth-century Gyeongbokgung Palace and the narrow alleyways of Bukchon Hanok Village. The group was led to a tram to go up Namsam Mountain to get a panoramic view of the city from rotating N Seoul Tower. As they drove along the Nami River banks, heading north to the Joint Security Area of the demilitarized zone, a diminutive woman from Miami sat in the front row of the tour bus.

Eddie called Eunji the very next day, and they found many common interests. She introduced him to K-pop music and eating bulgogi, and he helped her with her English and understanding American politics and culture. Eunji lived at home and was studying cosmetology and business to start her own upscale aesthetics shop. Her father was a successful businessman who owned a very popular bowling alley next to the Louis Vuitton store in the bustling, upscale Gangnam district. He was very protective of his three daughters. Most of their dates were either in groups or "chaperoned" by her friends or sisters. She had taken a purity pledge to remain a virgin until marriage, and Eddie's celibate status made him a perfect potential partner.

With Mochi's help, Eddie found a job he absolutely loved: doing copy transfer work for a film production company based in Seoul and Los Angeles. He was an intern, and it didn't pay much, but he was good at it and, for the first time in his life, got to be a part of something bigger than himself. It also helped that by having a job he could show Eunji's family that he could someday take care of her.

Eddie also used his spare time to research records from the Korean adoption agency. They wouldn't reveal his birth mother's identity, but he did learn that his original adopted parents were not the Vickersons but a Portland couple named Zapolski. Determined to find his twin-sister, he returned to the house in Tigard after New Year's Day, where he discovered that his soon-to-be ex-sister-in-law was now living in his bedroom. She was still traumatized by the fire and the breakup. Barb gave him the last pieces of information he needed to track down his twin sister, who had been living in Medford all along.

Karen cried when she saw Eddie for the first time since he was four. She explained the difficult decision she had to make to escape her violent husband with her twins and an even more difficult decision to separate them and leave her precious four-year-old boy to be raised by another family who could afford his healthcare, with Jerry's union healthcare policy coverage for family members.

She tearfully explained that it was the only choice she could make for the three of them. Barb had periodically secretly sent her pictures and information on Eddie, but had not told the full story of his struggles with drugs and his identity. She assured him that if she had known and felt that he could forgive her, she would have gone back for him.

Eddie struggled between competing emotions - anger at learning that he was abandoned by two different mothers and the joy at finally connecting with his sister. He decided that, for that moment, he needed most to hold on to Jennifer, the female reflection of himself that had been missing for nineteen years.

CHAPTER 12

A BRAND-NEW DAY

The sweet smell of hibiscus and a warm afternoon breeze greeted Evan as he stepped outside into the fresh air at Miami International Airport. He spotted his Uber driver, who took him to the downtown Marriott Residence Inn where John Paolo had made a reservation for him. Not luxurious, but a definite upgrade from the Stratford Inn. Once he checked in, he walked the few short blocks to the Regency Tower, the high-rise luxury condo where John Paolo and his mother lived. He walked into the condo's marble lobby and checked in with the desk attendant.

He took the elevator to the 57th-floor penthouse. The door opened into the foyer of an apartment that belonged to the scion of the Stinson family export business. A maid greeted him and escorted him through the double doors into the living room that looked like a hotel lobby with marble and brass and white leather sofas, fresh flowers in huge porcelain vases. Seated in a large animal print chair was the humble woman he met almost a year and a half ago in Khajuraho.

"Evan, thank you so much for coming all the way to Miami. We were getting worried when we didn't hear back from you. I read about the wildfires," she said.

"Yes, last year was kind of a rough year. I lost my home, my marriage, my lover, my connection to my parents and brother, and my job," he said.

"I'm so sorry," she said, "I have also landed myself in a bit of a pickle. It seems that the family of one of the doctors who died suddenly took an interest in the inheritance after the hateful parents died. But the bright side is that all the publicity about the case brought me back to my son."

John Paolo entered the room and added graciously, "And it brought me back to my mother. Hello, Mr. Vickerson, I have heard so much about you." John Paolo extended his hand with a firm grip, looking deep into Evan's eyes, as though he were a hypnotist casting a spell. Then his face broke into a big grin that showed all of his perfect white teeth. "May I offer you a drink?" he said.

"It's Evan, and scotch on the rocks, please." He found himself tripping over words. "I mean, call me Evan, and I'll drink Chivas if you have it." Evan rarely drank anymore and never in the afternoon, but he was so unhinged by the introduction to John Paolo that he babbled off the first thing that came to his mind. The tall, handsome, sophisticated man standing before him perfectly matched the smooth sexy voice that seduced him to travel to Miami.

"And you must call me J.P.," John Paolo said. Wanda smiled, knowingly.

John Paolo was vice president of marketing at Stinson Enterprises and poured his money into the condo and sports cars. He grew up in luxury and comfort in an exclusive section of Coral Gables, but finding his birth mother always nagged at him. Watching the family of a close friend whose mother died during the pandemic made him even more sensitive to how much he missed that maternal connection.

He hired a private investigator, who led him to Wanda on the day of her arrest. He paid her bail and moved her into one of the bedrooms in his condo. They became fast friends eager to make up for all the years that they had missed. He was fluent in French and enjoyed practicing it with her. He loved hearing her stories about exotic travel, growing up in France and Brazil, and working for a gay couple in Miami Beach. She wanted to hear all about the years she missed with him and how he had become such an impressive, caring man.

Wanda's trial was scheduled in Dade County Superior Court on the next day. She was charged with bank fraud, theft, and grand larceny for illegally using the funds from the off-shore accounts to pay for her lodging and travel. The team of lawyers that John Paolo hired entered a not guilty plea at the arraignment and planned a vigorous defense. The adult nephew of one of the doctors initiated the investigation to track down his uncle's fortune, though the rest of his family still wanted nothing to do with it. Most of the fortune remained intact, as Wanda had only used a small amount of the interest on the money to pay for her trips and upkeep of the house.

Evan sat next to a nervous John Paolo in the courtroom. Given that he had only known his mother for a few months, it was amazing how devoted he was. Perhaps it was the same spell that fell over Evan when he met her in Khajuraho.

The trial took just two days, and during court breaks, they would huddle in the hallway with Wanda and the lawyers. Evan made a few suggestions, but he was way out of his league. An accountant testified to the sheer financial size of the estate and the nephew gave a teary account of how he never got to know his wonderful uncle and his partner. Other witnesses spoke of how Wanda had tricked a wealthy family into supporting her, then illegally used the doctors' fortune to travel the world and live a carefree life of comfort and opulence.

It didn't look good for her when the prosecution rested their case. The defense called a couple of expert witnesses and in closing arguments made the case that she had merely served as a custodian to the property until someone else claimed rightful possession or the State took control of it. A psychologist testified about the emotional toll and the post-traumatic stress of families of 9/11 victims.

The jury deliberated for just one hour and returned to deliver the verdict. When the judge asked the foreman to read the verdict, John Paolo reached over and took Evan's hand, squeezing it tightly. Evan was a little shocked since they had only just met but didn't object, holding on tight to show support. The verdict was guilty on all the charges.

Wanda did not testify during the trial, but the judge gave her an opportunity to make a statement before sentencing. Her lawyers tried to discouraged her, but she assured them that she had seen enough Perry Mason episodes to plead her own case.

"Your honor, I realize that what I did was wrong," she said, "As the District Attorney has rightfully said, I should have vacated my employers' home and surrendered it to the State of Florida to decide how to handle this estate. But, you see, when they were alive, Saul and Demitri made me feel like it was my home too, that they were my family. After they died in that horrible way, no one seemed to care about them or those possessions. Their families chose not to have a relationship with them when they were alive, simply because they chose to love someone of the same sex. Even after their deaths, it took them eighteen years to claim them as part of their bloodline, to say that they were connected to them in life and death. And even now, it's only because of the money that they can get. I honor their memory and keep their memory alive in everything I do. I have told their story hundreds of times to people all over the world, saying proudly that they were two kind and honorable gay men and they were my friends. Once again, I acknowledge and apologize for the harm that I may have caused and accept whatever punishment you deem appropriate. I am a modest middle-aged woman and I did not squander their fortune or ransack their house. It is exactly as they left it in September of 2001. There is one more thing that I would ask you to kindly consider. For the past twenty-seven years, due to no fault of my own, I was separated from the son that I gave birth to. This case has brought him back into my life and for that I am truly grateful. I have never known a love so enduring and so patient. I ask only that you take as little time as possible away from my true inheritance, the precious time that I can spend with my only son."

The judge was sympathetic to Wanda and after a brief recess, returned to the courtroom to pronounce a very lenient six-month sentence to be served in a minimum-security prison near Miami, plus a fine and restitution of the funds she had taken from the estate. Wanda sobbed with relief and John Paolo rushed up to hug and console her.

Wanda had just two days to put her affairs in order before surrendering to the court. The three of them had dinner together back at the condo. Evan felt honored to have become part of this new-found family. Despite what had happened in court that day, they managed to have a pleasant evening together.

John Paolo explained to Evan during dinner that he was raised by his paternal grandparents after they paid off Wanda. His father Howard's name was on his birth certificate but they had somehow managed to have the mother's name removed. Howard was more interested in women and gambling and never showed much interest in the business nor in his son.

"Dad always brought a new girlfriend home to live with us and he always introduced the string of beautiful young women as my potential new mother. I learned not to ask my grandparents about my birth mother. They would always say that she wasn't able to take care of me, but reassured me that they always would be there for me."

"They told you that I had abandoned you to your father. That breaks my heart," Wanda said, "When they took you away, the attorney told me that they would make sure that you were given to a good family, but I had no idea that the Stinsons would raise you themselves. That you were just a few miles away from me all that time. If I had known, I would have come back for you.

I promise you that I would. And now I am abandoning you again."
She began to cry.

"I know, Mom, I know that you would have and this is just
a separation for a little while. We'll be here when you get back."
He looked over at Evan and let her cry for a little until she
composed herself. "My grandparents are good people, I just wish
they had told me the truth. They were kind and loving to me
growing up and gave me every material thing that I could ever
want. They encouraged me to be true to myself and pushed me to
be successful at school, paying for private tutors and elite schools.
In college, I put everything into my studies and graduated with
honors from business school at Vanderbilt. When I came back to
Miami, grandpa gave me a job heading up the marketing
department of Stinson Enterprises. I have been very lucky in life."

He wanted to change the subject and hear more about Evan.
Evan told them about growing up in Tigard, his very traditional
middle-class parents, and settling down with Sheila in Talent after
college. He described life in the verdant Rogue Valley, the
wonderful theater company that was resident there, the lakes,
mountains, hiking, the vineyards, and his quirky friend Darlene
who had gotten him into yoga and meditation. They laughed about
the weird names of yoga poses like downward dog. Wanda
yawned, bid good night, and excused herself. After one more glass
of Chivas, John Paolo asked, "Is Darlene your girlfriend?"

"Oh goodness, no," said Evan, "In fact, you might say that she's the wife of my former boyfriend."

"I was hoping that she wasn't," he said. The two men smiled broadly.

When he got back to the Marriott, there was a message for him at the front desk to "call your brother." He hadn't talked to Eddie since that night at his parent's home after returning from India. He dialed the number on the slip, and a happy guy with his brother's voice answered the phone.

"Hi, bro, how's it going? You're a hard guy to track down. All the way down in Miami."

"I'm good. Are mom and dad OK?" Evan asked, fearing that he must have bad news to share.

"Oh no, they're fine. Your evil ex-wife is making sure of that. I'm here in Medford. Sorry that I have been incommunicado, but I have some excellent news. I'm getting married in June to a great girl that I have been dating, and I would love it if you could come to the wedding."

"That's great, Eddie, but I think I missed a few beats here. The last I heard, you moved to Seoul."

"That's right. Just like you told me, I needed to find my destiny, and as soon as I got to Korea, I started to come alive, bro. My buddy Mochi got me into the film industry. I met my fiancée at a Boba shop. But there's more. When I was there, I went to the adoption agency and tracked down my twin sister and my first adopted mom. They were living here in Medford all along, and we spent the last few days getting to know each other, but really, it's like Jennifer and I were never separate, if you know what I mean. We look alike and think alike. And Karen is pretty cool too, once I got to know her. She feels bad for what she did but did what she had to do to keep us all safe. And now we're all together, and they are both coming to Korea with me as soon as possible. I want Jennifer to know what it's like to 'feel normal' too."

They talked for a while about the details of the wedding and Eddie's career. Finally, Eddie asked, "How about you, man. Are you doing, OK? What are you doing in Miami? There must be somebody pretty special down there."

"You know, I think there might well be," Evan responded.

It was Wanda's last day of freedom, and John Paolo told Evan that he had several special surprises for her. He just told her to dress elegantly and warmly. They took the town car to meet Evan at Ceccones Restaurant, tucked in the courtyard of a trendy

South Beach boutique hotel. She used to go there for their lavish Sunday brunches with the gay doctors. It was a beautiful sunny day, and John Paolo insisted that they only talk about happy things. Evan raised a glass of mimosa and made a toast "to adventures - past, present, and future!"

After brunch, they walked along the boardwalk, admiring the art deco hotels, arm-in-arm-in-arm. Wanda, in the center, felt protected by the two men who meant so much to her. They arrived at the boat dock at the end of the boardwalk and walked up to a beautiful chartered sports yacht with the moniker "Mr. Peeps" on its hull.

"How did you know?" Evan said as tears welled in his eyes.

"A good marketer always knows how to do his research to win the client," John Paolo said. They climbed aboard the yacht and spent the sunny afternoon sailing out into the Atlantic and zipping around Biscayne Bay. The captain found a secluded cove where Evan and John Paolo could snorkel in the aquamarine water, marveling at all the colorful fish and coral. They returned to the boat and sailed away. They dried off and relaxed on deck chairs with a couple of pina coladas while Wanda chatted with the captain.

"When did you know that you were gay? You seem so comfortable with it. It sort of fits you like a second skin," Evan asked.

"Oh, probably since I was five years old. I always knew that I was gay and came out in high school. There was even a gay-straight alliance group at my school. My grandparents were incredibly supportive. There were many open gays and lesbians in their elite social circle. Let's just say I had lots of uncles and aunties who were excellent role models."

"Did you have boyfriends in high school?" Evan asked.

"I had a few crushes, but I was kinda shy about approaching guys back then. My best friend Lance and I went to prom with our lesbian friend Charlene. Lance was straight or questioning, I'm not sure. The three of us were committed to making a statement, but it wasn't romantic. I did better at Vanderbilt. I met Jack on an app and we were together for about a year, but I guess I just wasn't ready yet for a long-term relationship, so we called it off. Since then, it's been all about the career and an occasional date, just to see what's out there."

"It's hard to believe that you were a shy kid. You own every room that you walk into," Evan said, "I wish I had a thimble full of your self-confidence." John Paolo smiled.

"So how about you? I guess this is all pretty new to you?" John Paolo asked.

"Sheila was my first and only girlfriend. We were married for six years. I never even thought about same sex attraction until I met this guy back in Oregon. I guess I was a late bloomer, but I have no regrets. I know now that this is who I was meant to be. It's just too bad that the guy who helped me come out wasn't at the same place that I was," Evan said.

"Life is funny. Sometimes when we don't get what we want, it's because there is something so much better waiting for us just around the corner," John Paolo said and Evan smiled.

When they entered to the condo, they discovered that John Paolo had arranged yet another surprise. The apartment was filled with fresh flowers and glowing candles for Wanda's farewell. A classical pianist sat at the baby grand serenading them, while a private chef served a three-course gourmet dinner, topped off with flaming cherries jubilee. They laughed about the wonderful day together and talked about the future when Wanda was free.

As her eyelids started getting heavy from all the sun and liquor she had taken in on that day, Wanda said, "Thank you, boys, for a wonderful day and evening. Memories that will make the next six months go by just a little faster. I better turn in now and get my last night of sleep on a pillow-top mattress. I have a feeling there won't be any of those where I'm going." She planted kisses on the cheeks to Evan and John Paolo.

As soon as her bedroom door closed, John Paolo took Evan's hand and led him out to the living room balcony where there watched a breathtaking view of the twinkling city lights and the bay, a full moon hanging low in the sky. He put his arms around Evan and gave him a long, deep kiss.

"I have been wanting to do that all day," John Paolo said. They stood there on the balcony for a while, watching the lights on the boats in the bay and kissed some more.

"I think we should call it a night," Evan said reluctantly, "Wanda is going to need you tomorrow and I need a little time to…"

"Of course, you are right. There is no rush, and besides," John Paolo said, "I know where you live." They both laughed and hugged a quick goodbye.

On the next morning, John Paolo took Wanda to the Sherriff's office at the courthouse and said his teary goodbyes. He stood there as the deputy took her away and walked down a long corridor. Wanda turned and gave a little wave and a wink.

Over the next six months, he visited her two or three times a week – sometimes alone and sometimes with Evan. A week after she went to prison, Evan checked out of the Marriott and moved into John Paolo's condo. They took things slowly at first, but were rarely apart during the next few months. John Paolo constantly surprised Evan with romantic gestures and extemporaneous displays of affection.

Evan found a job managing an art gallery in South Beach. He liked meeting the artists and had a knack for arranging exhibitions and opening nights. He revived his talent for singing from high school choir days and joined the Miami Gay Men's Chorus. In the Chorus, he met some older guys who had been part of the two gay doctors' inner circle, and they fondly remembered Wanda. Apparently, she had become a bit of a folk hero in the gay community through the gay media, which covered her case favorably and rallied support for her. They seemed to know already that she was supportive of her gay son.

That June, Evan and John Paolo flew to Seoul, for Eddie and Eunji's wedding, attended by over a hundred of Eunji's well-connected family and friends, along with Karen and Jennifer. Evan was the proud best man, and John Paolo was a groomsman along with Mochi. Barb, Jerry, and Sheila participated remotely via a live video stream connection, and a large television screen projected them into the ceremony.

The wedding was held in an event center that was part of the bride's family's bowling alley. After the ceremony, the whole bowling alley was taken over by the wedding party. The new couple took separate lanes and formed teams that led their groomsmen and bridesmaids in a friendly ten pin competition.

CHAPTER 13

SAPLINGS EMERGE

A few weeks after the wedding, Evan got up the courage to call Sheila on the Fourth of July, the first time that they had spoken since the divorce was finalized in March. He hoped that the holiday would put her in a good mood. She had just popped some homemade Jamaican roti and meat pies in the oven when the phone rang.

"Hi Sheila, this is Evan," he said.

"Hello, Evan. I saw you at Eddie's wedding. Sorry, we couldn't make it, but Jerry and Barb don't travel much. You looked well. Is that guy you were with your…uh? Are you together?"

"Yes, that's J.P., we live together in Miami." Evan paused, not sure if it was helpful to add more details. "How about you? Are you seeing anyone?"

"No," Sheila lied, not quite ready to tell the man who had broken her heart that she had met someone special and that his two daughters were in the next room reading Harry Potter books.

" I'm calling because some legal documents related to the fire were returned. Do you have a new address?"

"Yes, I am sharing a house with Karen now in Northeast Portland. After I moved out of your parent's house, I had a small apartment downtown for a little while, but it felt lonely. When Karen's husband died in prison, she discovered that he left everything to her, including this four-bedroom house. The neighborhood is not great, but the house is a huge Victorian that we're slowly renovating and modernizing. She moved up here and started a small daycare business for low-income single mothers. Jennifer comes up to help during semester breaks and I help out when I can. The house is always full of delightful little rascals. We're having a holiday picnic in the back yard for them and their moms today."

"That's wonderful, Sheila," he said, "I'm really happy for you, and perhaps we will see you at Christmas." He took down her new address.

"Funny story," he said, "the guy that I'm living with is the son of Wanda, the woman we met in India." But she had already hung up and begun attending to the beef and chicken pastries in the oven.

It had been a painful nine months for Sheila since the Almeda wildfire. She spent many months feeling numb, being enraged at Evan and then feeling sorry for herself. She slowly realized that for all of her life, what she feared the most was being alone and she clung to the Vickerson clan for much longer than she needed to. As she read the divorce papers just before signing them, it occurred to her that she had always defined marriage as self-sacrifice, not love or partnership. That was the example that she had learned from her own mother and from Barb.

What turned things around for her was her new job. For the first time in her life, she had a sense of self-confidence, a clear purpose, and power as the leader of a group of mostly male techies. She was smarter than them, worked harder than them and the work was rewarding. She was quickly promoted to be the first woman vice-president in the company's history and she became a mentor to other women in tech. She could actually see her ideas go from the boardroom to consumer products that improved people's lives. There was more to her than just being Evan's wife and Barb's favorite daughter-in-law.

Sheila fell in love with Leia and Precious before she met Rodney. They were 6 and 8 years old, and their mother died of breast cancer four years before. Rodney worked two jobs to help pay off his wife's medical bills - as an Uber driver at night and as a clerk at the Mark Spencer Hotel during the day. He was the only single father whose kids were in Karen's daycare center. Sheila adored the girls, braiding their silky hair, playing patty-cakes and jump rope, and giving them books to read.

One day, when Rodney was late getting off work, she finally met this tall, muscular Jamaican man, who did such wonderful things with the English language when he spoke with that lilting accent.

"I'm sorry, Miss Sheila," he said, "I had a fare who took me plumb out to the airport before he realized that he forgot his suitcase. I always get here to pick the girls up on time, but tonight I just could not make it." The girls came running out of the house, screaming, "Daddy, Daddy." He scooped them up in his big arms and gave them big kisses. "I promise that I will make it up to you and Miss Karen."

"Well, you can start by calling me Sheila, Rodney," she said.

"The girls just adore you, and they talk about the wonderful Miss Sheila all the time. Nice to finally meet you. I had no idea that you were so young and beautiful." Sheila blushed.

"Perhaps I could make it up to you with dinner with us tonight? Have you eaten?" The girls started jumping up and down, screaming, imploring Sheila to say "yes." She learned that night that Rodney was not only persuasive and charming but a wonderful chef who loved spending time in the kitchen as much as she did, though he could have turned down the spice a bit for Sheila's taste.

Soon Sheila was tutoring him for his citizenship test but found that he knew much more about U.S. history and civics than she did. They went out for dinner or to dance clubs alone a few times, but what they both enjoyed most was time with the girls. She enjoyed reading bedtime stories to them and then cuddling up on the couch with Rodney afterward. He told wonderful stories about his crazy childhood in Jamaica and sad, sad stories about his wife and her time of a year-long struggle with breast cancer. She was French Canadian from Montreal, where they married and then moved together to Portland right before Precious was born. He had little time to grieve between raising two daughters, working two jobs, and studying for his citizenship class.

The man was always on the move and yet found time to let Sheila know how much she meant to him and genuinely listen to her in a way that no man had ever done. Despite the pressures of her new job, she knew that growing in love with Rodney and his family was the most important thing she had ever done in her life.

Leia squirmed around on Sheila's lap during the U.S. Courthouse naturalization ceremony, while Precious fell asleep leaning against her. Rodney's aunt and brother sat next to them, beaming with pride when they heard Rodney's name called, and cheering as he marched across the stage to receive his citizenship certificate from the U.S. Senator. Precious turned to Sheila after the applause died down, waving her American flag, and said, "Daddy's an American now, just like us."

After the ceremony, they gathered with other families in the Great Hall for a family portrait that put Rodney in the center, his arms around Sheila and the girls in front. It was their first family portrait and the first of many to come, Sheila hoped.

A couple of days later, Sheila was putting that picture into Rodney's family album. She saw his wedding photo with his late wife and birth photos of the girls. She noticed an older picture of a family group that she didn't recognize and asked Rodney who they were.

"Those are my grandparents, my father, and his siblings," He said, "They took that at the Christ the Redeemer statue when they lived in Rio, right before they moved to Kingston, where my grandfather was the French Ambassador. That's where my father met and married my mother. The boy next to my father is my Uncle Pierre who lives in Louisville now."

"But who is the girl?" Sheila asked, "It's not your Aunt Tessie."

"No, Aunt Tessie is my mother's sister." Rodney said, "The girl in the picture has always been a bit of a mystery. She was adopted and only lived with them for a couple of years. I think she disappeared or something when they were living in Rio." Sheila turned the picture over and read the meticulously written inscription "The Sambocars in Rio 1988 Francois, Violette, Hernan, Pierre and ..." The last name, which had been inelegantly scratched out, was "Wanda."

CHAPTER 14

FLOW, FLOWING, FLOWN

John Paolo returned to the Miami condo from work on a hot September evening and brought in the mail. He kissed Evan and handed him a formal envelope addressed to "Mr. Evan Vickerson and Mr. John Paolo Stinson" with a Tigard return address. Inside he found an engraved invitation to Barb and Jerry's 35th wedding anniversary celebration in early November. There was a handwritten note that said, "It's time we met your friend and welcomed him to the family. Love you, son." The handwriting was Jerry's. Evan began to cry.

He immediately called Barb to ask what had turned his father around. He hadn't spoken to Jerry in almost a year and he couldn't remember his father ever saying that he loved him, much less acknowledge his sexuality.

"Believe it or not, it was your brother," she said, "When he and Eunji call from Korea, he can't stop talking about you and that fellow. It sounds like he's pretty devoted to you. We read that book you gave us, and it didn't all make sense to us, but the way Eddie talks about you made us realize that we are missing out on your life and that it's a happy time for you."

"It really is, Mom. I can't wait for you to meet John Paolo." He told her a little bit about their lives together in Miami.

"Also," she said, then added after a dramatic pause, "once your father found out that Shephard Smith on Fox News was gay, he softened up a bit, asked more questions, and even went to a PFLAG meeting with me. He's not all the way there yet, but he's getting there. Even with Eddie, he's a lot more patient and really proud about the man he has become. He's always telling his buddies that his son's father-in-law owns a classy bowling alley in Korea. This will be our thirty-fifth year of marriage, honey. We talked about it and decided that what is most important is to have all of our family here - you and Eddie and your spouses and Sheila and her family. After this past year of so much turmoil and the pandemic, when we couldn't all get together, it just feels right to be with all of our very perfect children."

"And how about Sheila? Is she O.K. with John Paolo coming?" Evan asked.

"I already spoke with her and she wholeheartedly wants both of you here," she said, "The girls are growing up so quickly. They are going to leave them with us while they are on their honeymoon. For some reason, they decided to do it with a group tour company. To save money, I guess. They're going to Patagonia just before Halloween. Do you want to speak to your father?" Barb asked. Evan declined and wanted some time to let all the good news sink in and he also remembered that he had something in the oven that might need his attention.

He pulled the lasagna out of the oven just in the nick of time, before going to the bedroom to tell John Paolo about the conversation with his mother. He found his boyfriend lying across the king-size bed, watching an episode of Law and Order SVU. Before he could open his mouth to talk about his conversation with Barb, a familiar face came on the screen as the reluctant witness to the sexual assault of a female exchange student.

"Oh my God, that's Gregory!" Evan exclaimed, "Darlene told us that he would be on the show at some point this month." Evan sat on the bed and they watched the episode together.

Once the television was off, Evan did a recap of his conversation with his mother and they went to kitchen to finish preparing dinner. Evan discovered a passion for cooking simple dishes that he must have absorbed from watching Sheila over the years. As they enjoyed the Italian meal, they began to make plans to travel back to Oregon in November. John Paolo suggested they go early and stopover in southern Oregon and the wheels started turning for a surprise thirty-fourth birthday celebration at a rental cabin at the Lake of the Woods.

John Paolo met Gregory when they went to Ashland in late July to see him perform the lead role in *Pericles* at OSF. He was just a tiny bit jealous, knowing his history with Evan. The show was a sold-out hit with a prolonged standing ovation that night. It was John Paolo's first time in a small town and he was impressed to see the vitality, with tourists flocking back to see professional theater and visit the wineries.

Darlene joined them for diner at Beasley's on the Creek before the show and he felt this instant connection to her. Of course, Evan had told him a lot about his gal pal, but it was as though they had known each other before. There was something eerily familiar about her that he couldn't quite put his finger on.

They had stayed at an Airbnb in Talent while they were visiting the Rogue Valley for Gregory's show Evan showed John Paolo around his old hometown and they saw only a few signs of the destruction that had occurred the year before. There were lots of new pre-fab homes and new vegetation, flowers and trees where only ashes once stood. A new home stood at 315 Strawberry Lane with a Radio Flyer red wagon and a girl's bicycle on the front lawn, next to a yellow rose bush in full bloom.

On the morning of Wanda's return home from prison (or lady prison, as they liked to call it), Evan got up early to make a healthy breakfast which he served on the balcony. John Paolo had taken the day off work. One of their favorite new traditions was watching the sunrise together. They held hands across the bistro table feeling incredibly grateful to have found each other.

Evan went for a five-mile run along the Miami Riverwalk while John Paolo went to the Dade County Sheriff's Office to pick up his mother. Wanda returned from lady prison to a busy home filled with life, including a sassy new white Persian Himalayan cat named Krishna. John Paolo had settled her fine to the court and paid all her legal fees. She was a free woman again.

For so many years she had been alone among strangers, wandering about the world on her own, sitting in the front of the bus to see everything outside, while not connecting to the people behind her. For so many years she returned to a beautiful but empty house of sad memories, with no one that she could share her adventures and discoveries. There were only two times in her fifty-six years that she had truly felt part of a loving family: once with the gay doctors and now with her son and his lover.

John Paolo loved pampering her and surprising her with little gifts and gestures. While she appreciated it, somehow it didn't feel like she was living the life that she was meant to live anymore.

After a couple of weeks at the condo, she began to feel that it was the right time to give her boys some space. They were still getting to know each other and needed to settle into their own rhythm. Also, being cooped up in a jail cell for six months had made her restless, and she had the urge to wander again.

In early October, she announced that she was going on a group tour but wouldn't say where she was going. She had traveled to over fifty countries, and whenever the guys asked where she was going, she would say that she hadn't decided yet and would pull out another Smartours brochure to ask their opinion. She left the impression that Jordan and Petra, Easter Island, and Patagonia were on the top of her list. The tour company remembered her well and booked her immediately into the very next escorted group tour. She promised to let Evan and John Paolo know her destination on the day of her departure.

Two weeks passed quickly and the day of her departure arrived. The guys kept busy planning their own trip for the anniversary celebration. They drove her to the airport and dropped her off at curbside. She went to the American Airlines ticket counter and checked her bags, while the guys parked the car in the airport garage.

Evan and John Paolo stood with their arms around each other in the vast concourse of Miami International Airport, ready to say farewell for Wanda's departure on her big trip. She was ready to leave her boys and go through the security check towards a new adventure.

She took Evan's hand into her own, looked into his eyes, and asked him to promise her three things, "Take care of my son, give me beautiful grandchildren and make sure that J.P. goes to the Taj Mahal someday." As they laughed, she hugged them both and turned to go through the security gate.

"Wait, Mom," John Paolo called out, "you never told us where the group tour is going or when you'll be back." She gave them a wicked grin, a wink, a wave, and walked away.

THE END (…maybe)

ABOUT THE AUTHOR

 Lorenz Qatava resides in Ashland Oregon and Palm Springs California. He graduated with a degree in International Affairs from Georgetown University and in Public Health from the University of Minnesota. He retired recently after 30 years working for the federal government in international cultural affairs, health-related social marketing in developing countries, and public health policy. He is an avid fan of live theater and has traveled to more than 40 countries, often on group tours. This is his first novel.

www.ingramcontent.com/pod-product-compliance
Lightning Source LLC
Chambersburg PA
CBHW052043150726

48002CB00002B/724